REACHING OUT FROM THE COLD
DARKNESS UNDER THE BED, THE
INTRUDER'S GLOVED HAND
SURROUNDED MAX'S THIN WRIST AND
HAULED HIM FORWARD. . . .

He was here! Max realized. *He was here all the time!*

Max tried to pull away, but the hand was too strong. As he screamed, the intruder laughed: a raspy dry cackle.

Max yanked free and fell backward, landing hard on the rug.

From under the bed, the hand grabbed his ankle. Max drew in a quick gasp.

The hand had no skin.

It was the bony hand of a living skeleton. The hard strong fingers pressed into his flesh and yanked him forward.

Max tried to kick free, but something felt wrong. He glanced down under the bed and saw his feet dissolving into nothingness.

Get me out of this! Somebody, please, get me out of this!

From the chilly darkness, Max heard a rough crackling voice. "Give it up, boy. Come with me. . . ."

ARE YOU AFRAID OF THE DARK?™ novels

The Tale of the Sinister Statues
The Tale of Cutter's Treasure

Available from MINSTREL Books

NICKELODEON™

Are You Afraid of the Dark?™

THE TALE OF
CUTTER'S TREASURE

Based on the teleplay by Chloe Brown

DAVID L. SEIDMAN

A MINSTREL® BOOK

PUBLISHED BY POCKET BOOKS

New York   London   Toronto   Sydney   Tokyo   Singapore

A MINSTREL PAPERBACK *Original*

 A Minstrel Book published by
POCKET BOOKS, a division of Simon & Schuster Inc.
1230 Avenue of the Americas, New York, NY 10020

ISBN: 0-671-52729-0

First Minstrel Books printing May 1995

10 9 8 7 6 5 4 3 2 1

Cover photography by Mark Malabrigo and Jonathan Wenk

Printed in the U.S.A.

To my parents, Marvin and Seena,
who put up with two boys of their own—
and a girl, too.

THE TALE OF
CUTTER'S TREASURE

Prologue: The Midnight Society

Come closer. I know it's dark out here in the woods, but don't be afraid. No one's going to hurt you.

Take a seat by the campfire. Tonight, you're one of us. You're a member of the Midnight Society.

When we meet around this fire to tell our tales, each of us has his or her own special brand of terror. Some of us tell stories of adventure. Others have tales of the macabre and grotesque. Some tell stories about real people trapped in an unreal world, or about heroes searching for the truth.

And then there's Rush.

Like any other teenager, Rush wanted to run his life without interference. There was only one problem: his little brother, Max. Max wanted to hang around with Rush, but Rush—well, he didn't want a kid tagging along underfoot. Rush thought he could handle anything without anybody's help. Until the pirates rose from the dead.... But we're getting ahead of ourselves here.

Both Gary and Frank are going to tell tonight's tale. It's too big for just one of us. You see, it has magic ... and mayhem! It's about an evil power so strong that it survived for centuries, waiting to spread its terror....

So what are we waiting for?

Submitted for the approval of the Midnight Society, we call this story ...

The Tale of Cutter's Treasure.

CHAPTER 1

Only one of us will leave this room alive, Ian Keegan thought.

With a soft creak, a thick door of heavy oak angled open in a rocky wall. Seaman First Class Keegan eased his hand into a vast cavern, holding a needle-sharp dagger. He peered through the doorway with wide, staring eyes. It was good to send the dagger in ahead of his body. A guard might be waiting by the door. Or worse, Captain Cutter might be waiting. Keegan took a slow, trembling breath to calm his fluttering heart.

He was no coward. In the stone tunnels that led to this room, he had already fought Mr. Noise. Cutter's gleeful, wheezing first mate terrified

3

every sailor from the Dutch East Indies to the China Seas with his talent for ambushing the unsuspecting. He had jumped Keegan from an offshoot of the tunnel and wrapped his clawlike hands around Keegan's throat—but when their struggle was over, Keegan had left Mr. Noise bleeding on the tunnel's rocky floor.

But now Keegan gulped hard and nearly gagged; his throat felt as dry as parchment. Although a chandelier of twenty candles warmed the air, he shivered.

He glanced about the cave, watching for trouble, listening for movement. No sound came from the dank stone walls. No sound came from the heaps of shining treasure strewn about the floor: doubloons, jewels, paintings, and other loot from missions of plunder. No sound came from the tall straight-backed chair at the center of the chamber, or from the murderer who sat quietly as Keegan entered.

The chair sat with its back to Keegan. In the chair was a figure wearing a captain's hat. Cutter had stolen the hat from the first captain he'd killed and claimed it as his own.

Keegan approached the figure in the chair silently. He and Cutter had been shipmates on the *Queen's Ransom*—until Cutter led a band of mutineers to take over the ship. Cutter dubbed him-

4

self captain, renamed the vessel *Cutter's Throne*, and claimed its cargo of gold and jewels as his own.

"You're a good man, Ian," Cutter had said. "Warm-hearted and honest, not a bit of cruelty in you." Cutter grinned. "That's why I like making you do bad things." At sword's point, Cutter forced Keegan to feed the crew to the sharks. Keegan could still see his friends drowning and hear their anguished screams.

When they returned to port, after a dozen missions of thievery and murder, Cutter took his treasure down to this room, while Keegan found the widows and orphans of the murdered men and promised to avenge them.

Within a foot of the chair, Keegan stopped. He raised his knife and whispered, "I use this dagger in the name of all who fell to yer sword, you devil." Still staring at the figure in the chair, Keegan kissed the blade and took a deep breath. *Careful, now*, he thought. *This is the moment.* He lunged for the chair and spun it around, ready to strike.

A skull leered back at him.

A skeleton sat upright in the chair, dressed in a captain's hat and uniform. *Tricked*, Keegan thought. He backed away. *Dear Lord, I have to get out of here!*

He heard a low, guttural chuckle.

He whirled. On a shadowy ledge deep within the stone wall stood a Persian throne—and in the throne sat Cutter, laughing. Holding a shining knife, he sliced a loaf of hard, crusty bread. On his index finger was a blue sapphire ring stolen from a crewman he had murdered.

"Hello, Ian," Cutter said with a growl. "Makin' a social call, are ya?"

Keegan backed away. Stumbling over a thick Persian rug, he fell to the floor. His knuckles hit the rocky floor, knocking the dagger out of his grip. It landed near the doorway behind him, in front of a table covered with an antique tapestry.

Lying on his back, Keegan knew that he had no way to escape. "I warn ya!" he cried. He could not keep his voice from shaking. "Others'll come."

"Let them!" Cutter grinned. He sawed through the bread, faster and harder. "I enjoy slicing into filthy traitors like yourself." He jammed the point of the knife into a nearby treasure chest.

A small boy slipped in through the doorway.

Everyone on the *Queen's Ransom* believed that Ian's son would someday make a fine spy. Young Eric Keegan loved to sneak into places deemed off-limits. He would eavesdrop on Ian's conversations or follow him to card games and steal his winnings, without letting Ian know that he'd even been in the room.

Eric, keeping out of Ian and Cutter's sight, silently hid behind the tapestry-covered table near the dagger. He watched the men, fascinated.

Keegan looked for his dagger, but it was not within reach. Only fast talk could save him now. "Too much innocent blood has been spilled for this treasure," he began.

"And there will be more!" Cutter shouted with glee. He bounded off the ledge and headed toward Keegan, while Eric grabbed his father's dagger and slipped out of the chamber unnoticed to get help. "I plan to guard my treasure until the day I die, Ian Keegan. Longer if need be."

"Then a curse upon you, Jonas Cutter," Keegan said. The captain's thick hand reached for a long saber hanging at his waist. Keegan stared at the sword with wide eyes. His voice quavered. "May this treasure never bring a moment's peace to your greedy soul."

"And may your death"—Cutter pulled the sword from its scabbard—"be a bloody one." Cutter raised the sword high. Keegan lifted his arms to cover his face as the pirate swung the blade down. . . .

CHAPTER 2

The blade swung down toward its target. Tony Conchelos screamed.

Nine-year-old Max Keegan's blade was green and hard and plastic. Max's best friend, Tony, dodged the toy and ran like a wildcat, clutching a plastic sword of his own.

"Arr! Come back here, ya scurvy dog!" Max commanded. He grinned and sprinted after Tony, chasing him across the wide front lawn of the Keegan home. Raising his sword high, Max declared, "I'll run ya through!"

Tony glanced over his shoulder. He caught a flash of sunlit grass and water—the Keegans' front lawn faced smooth, peaceful Prospect Sound—but

8

mostly he focused on Max. The boy in blue jeans and rainbow T-shirt was pounding across the lawn and catching up fast.

Tony turned and lunged at Max, lashing out with his own sword. The boys dueled, their blades bumping.

Suddenly, Max raised a silencing finger to his lips. Behind Tony, a girl was giggling. Slowly, the two boys crept around the tall hedge that separated the Keegans' front yard from the back. Sitting on a blanket in the back yard, awkwardly looking at the grass, at the blanket, at anything but each other, were Max's fourteen-year-old brother, Rush, and a chestnut-haired girl from Rush's school, Sandy Campbell. Quietly, the two boys crouched and watched.

Tony grinned at his friend. Max, however, was focused on his brother. He had never seen his brother with a girl before, and wondered what Rush would do.

As far as Max was concerned, Rush could handle anything. He had shown Max how to jump Graves' Gorge on a bicycle, how to sneak into movies for free, and how to climb the big fir tree in Prospect Park without falling. When Max ran away from home last year, it was Rush who knew where to find him, and in the winter, the two brothers could beat anyone in snowball fights.

9

But recently, Rush was less interesting in hanging out with Max. And now, he was alone with a girl. *Girls,* Max thought. *Yuck!*

Rush bit his lip, annoyed. *Say something,* he thought to himself. Sandy seemed to like him—so why couldn't he talk to her? Maybe it was because she was so pretty, with flawless skin and dark eyes; pretty girls made him nervous. He hadn't been this stuck for words since old Miss Van Nordling forced him to stand up in front of social studies class and tell how he felt about his country.

He grabbed an idea at random. "So, you wanna come over tonight?" The words tumbled out too quickly. *Darn,* he thought. *I've gotta sound more adult!* Sandy looked up at him, waiting for more. "And, uh, watch TV or something?" he added. *Not real adult. Well, I tried.*

"Sure," Sandy said. She looked down, blushing a little, and tried to hide her smile. Shyly, she added, "Sounds like fun." Rush beamed. *It worked!*

As the two spies watched the teenagers, Tony clapped a hand over his mouth, trying to hold back a fit of giggles. Max tapped him on the shoulder and pointed to a small metal object near Rush and Sandy. Tony looked at the thing and shook his head no.

10

Max nodded yes. He grabbed the collar of Tony's T-shirt and pulled. The two boys slipped quietly behind the hedge.

Rush tried to catch Sandy's eye. She was looking away from him, smiling nervously. The silence between them stretched on. *Come on,* he told himself. *Do something, you dork!*

Rush raised his hand off of the blanket, hesitated, then took Sandy's hand. Her skin felt warm, smooth, and soft. Her fingers didn't twitch or pull away; they stayed calmly in his.

A few yards away, another hand reached for a steel spigot.

Sandy was looking into Rush's eyes now, still smiling. She squeezed his hand gently and leaned in close. Rush bent toward her, closed his eyes, and opened his lips.

Cold water sprayed his face.

It kept coming, striking his chest and legs, and Sandy's as well. The two teenagers yelped, jumping to their feet. Someone had turned on a nearby lawn sprinkler.

"Arrrr! Victory!" Max leaped out from behind the hedge. He swung his plastic cutlass through the air and laughed, making a noise that, he hoped, sounded like a pirate's nasty cackle.

Rush groaned in frustration. Why did his creepy younger brother always have to spoil everything? "Max, you little—"

11

"I'm going home," Sandy said. She sounded hurt.

"Sandy, wait!" Rush protested. But she ran off and was gone.

Rush growled in frustration. He turned back to Max, who was still laughing as Tony jumped from the bushes to join him.

With tight fists, Rush ran straight as a bullet toward his brother. Max stopped laughing and shot back behind the hedge, still holding his toy sword. Tony split away and escaped from the property, heading for home.

Max whipped around the hedge. Ahead of him, across the front lawn, stood the broad red-brick face of the Keegan house.

In the driveway, he saw two adults piling water bottles, packages of dried fruit, and a bedroll into the family station wagon: Mom and Dad. They'd save him from Rush! Max ran forward, his feet tearing up the lawn.

Strong arms grabbed his shoulders and shoved him to the ground.

"You are dead, toe-jam!" Rush barked. "You are *never* going to ruin my life again." He grabbed Max's shirt front, his angry fingers nearly ripping through the fabric.

"Rush? Max?" called their father. "C'mon, we're outta here!"

12

"Hammer you later," Rush promised his brother. He shoved Max to the ground and ran toward the driveway. As he went, he made sure to stamp on the younger boy's plastic sword.

Max gasped for air. He stumbled to his feet to follow Rush.

The brothers jogged to a stop behind the station wagon. Two mountain bicycles, their wheels turning slowly in the slight breeze, lay strapped to the wagon's roof. The boys' mother—a trim, tanned woman in shorts, polo shirt, and sneakers—held a small envelope three inches in front of Rush's eyes. "Here's the check for Mrs. Gregory," she explained.

Gee, Mom, Rush thought, *You could just hand it to me. You don't have to treat me like some little kid who's never seen a check before.*

Mom ran a loving hand over Rush's hair and cheek with a gentle caress. He flinched at the smothering touch. With a warm smile, she strolled over to the car as Rush protested, "Aw, Mom, we don't need a babysitter. I'm old enough to handle things."

"Oh, really," Dad said. Rush and Max turned to see the tall, broad-chested man, dressed in the same athletic style as Mom, hanging casually on the car door. He regarded Rush with a skeptical half-smile. "Aren't you the guy that just yelled, 'You are dead, toe-jam'?"

13

Rush sighed. *Nailed. He's never going to treat me like a grownup. And it was all Max's fault!*

Dad slid into the driver's seat and strapped on his safety belt, while Mom spoke up through the window of the passenger-side door. "It's only for a couple of days. So be good." She paused for a moment to let the command sink in. "And wish us luck."

"Seventy-five miles a day, we're gonna need it," Dad added. He shut his door and started the car. Rush and Max watched the station wagon pull down the curved driveway and roll out of sight.

"Mrs. Gregory smells like fish," Max griped.

"Well, she's not stinkin' up my weekend," Rush said.

Like other houses on the shore of Prospect Sound, the Keegan home was decorated in a nautical style, down to the anchor-shaped knocker on the front door. An hour after Mom and Dad had left, a mottled hand took hold of the knocker and rapped three times.

No answer.

Mrs. Gregory—wrinkled, bespectacled, her thin lips pressed firmly into a permanent grimace—squinted through the door's peephole. The old woman saw the white-walled foyer of the Keegan house, but no people.

14

Near her waist, the door's mail slot flipped open with a metallic creak. "Mrs. Gregory?" came a deep voice. The old woman looked around.

"Down here," the voice continued.

Mrs. Gregory kneeled down to the slot. "Mr. Keegan? Is that you?"

Through the dark rectangular hole came the reply: "Uh, yes. I'm sorry, but we decided not to go away this weekend."

"Oh?" The voice on the other side of the door sounded too deep and over-emphasized every syllable, not like the easygoing Mr. Keegan at all. Perhaps the metallic mail slot distorted his voice.

"Yes, uh, the boys are sick." Now, why did Mr. Keegan hesitate? Could he be ill himself? That must be the reason why his voice sounded so odd.

Mrs. Gregory leaned forward. "Oh, well, I'm very good at taking care of—" A hand holding an envelope broke through the slot and poked toward Mrs. Gregory's face. Dozens of scarlet spots covered the hand. Mrs. Gregory scrambled backward, away from the repulsive, diseased fingers.

"They've got the measles," the voice from the slot continued. "Of course, we'll pay you anyway."

15

Mrs. Gregory reached forward, trembling, and snatched the envelope. "Thank you," she said, her voice quivering. "I hope you feel better soon." She fled with remarkable speed for a woman of her age. The spotted hand waved a cheery goodbye.

Inside the house, Max pulled his hand back through the mail slot. "Yes!" he and Rush hissed. Sitting in the foyer next to the door, they grinned widely and slapped a high five.

Max leaned eagerly toward his brother. "We're alone the whole weekend. What're we gonna do first?"

Rush's smile faded. He pulled back as if Max had suddenly developed a bad smell. "*We're* not doing anything," he answered. "*You've* done enough already to mess things up. You're on your own." He stood up and walked away.

Max's mouth fell open. He rose to follow Rush. "I thought we were a team."

"We *were* a team," Rush agreed, as he checked his hair in the early American mirror that hung on the foyer wall. *Looks good. Sandy'll love it.* He glanced at Max. "You just got cut."

Rush chuckled and headed to a small antique end table near the curtained front windows, where Mom had left the family's cellular phone. He picked up the phone and pulled out its an-

16

tenna. *Me, Sandy, a whole weekend—oh, yeah! Max is not going to get in the way this time....*

"Come on," Max said, getting annoyed. Rush wasn't being fair. "You said if I helped you, I could do whatever I want."

"You can," Rush replied, exasperated. "Go over to Tony's, stay up all night, I don't care. Just keep outta my face."

He strode away from Max, passed the stairway that led up to their bedroom, and entered the living room. Like the foyer and front door, the living room was decorated with antiques from the era of sailing ships. Paintings of stormy seas hung on the wall, and a miniature model of an old clipper stood on a credenza. The furniture dated from two centuries past, and even the fringed coverlet on the couch was old.

Max shook his head like a bull about to charge and followed his brother. "You cheated!" he protested. "I'm telling Mom you made me lie to Mrs. Gregory."

Rush whirled. *This has got to stop right now.* With a mean glare, he shoved the phone at his brother. Its antenna nearly hit Max in the face. Rush parked the black plastic tip on Max's chest. "You do and you're dead."

Max glared up at him. "Yeah? How're you gonna stop me?"

17

Rush opened his mouth to answer, then closed it. *What can I do? Maybe if I pound him—nah, he'd just tell Mom.* He sighed. "Okay, worm. What do you want?"

Max suddenly looked much younger and smaller. "I just wanna do something together," he said quietly.

Rush shook his head. "Forget it." He jumped over the back of the living-room couch and bounced on the seat cushions. "What else do you want?"

Max thought for a moment. He pulled a folded handbill from his back pocket. "There is something." He opened the paper and handed it to Rush. "This ad came in the mail yesterday."

It was a flimsy, yellowing thing, hand lettered in a crude style by an amateur. It began:

YOU CAN BE A **MAGICIAN**
YOU CAN DO TRICKS

Below the lettering was a drawing of a gypsy surrounded by flame. "Have the courage to walk through the portals of *Sardo's Magic Mansion*," the ad read, "for *Shandu's Magic Kit*."

Rush grimaced as if he'd just bitten into something sour. "A magic set?"

18

Max leaned over the back of the couch. He spoke directly into Rush's ear. "Get me that set, and I'll leave you alone all weekend."

Rush glanced over his shoulder at Max. *Are you serious?* He looked back at the ad. How much trouble could a magic kit cause?

CHAPTER

3

From the outside, only the doorway's plastic awning marked the Magic Mansion as unusual. In screaming tomato red, the awning displayed the shop's name, hand lettered (no doubt by the same amateur that had made the flyer) to look gooey and dripping.

Otherwise, nothing about the Magic Mansion's exterior indicated that it was different from any other store. The outer walls of stone brick were painted the same white as the other stores on Kelting Street; the doorway was an ordinary wooden rectangle with a glass pane to let customers see in; the window was filled with wands and top hats, just like any magic shop.

Inside was another story.

The room was dark, filled with strange artifacts. A hand projected out from a teakwood plaque, offering a poison apple. On the floor nearby stood a partially constructed wire-frame globe of a mysterious planet. Sticks of spiced incense stood in a jar, clogging the air with the sweet aroma of rotted roses. Crystal balls and dusty books weighed down weary, old shelves. Blood-dark rugs from a haunted house carpeted the floor; heavy curtains from Houdini's favorite theater lined the walls. Glass vials filled with gloomy elixirs stood on a cherrywood desk that must have weighed half a ton.

Behind the desk was Sardo the shopkeeper, a moon-faced man wearing a purple vest, a gypsy blouse of pink satin, and a golden earring. With his round body, pink skin, and dark piercing eyes, he resembled an especially sly and crafty barnyard pig.

The man held an eyedropper above a silver caldron that sat on a lighted glass pane set in the desktop. White fluid, thick as maple syrup and smelling like strawberries, filled the caldron.

As the light cast a glow over his smooth, jowly face, Sardo spoke with the tantalizing earnestness of an evangelist about to reveal the secrets that will bring his congregation to heaven. "This for-

21

mula is very old," he declared, "and very powerful."

Next to Sardo sat Rush, his forearm slung over a large wooden box whose lid displayed a picture of a tuxedoed man spreading out handfuls of playing cards: the Shandu magic kit. Rush watched, fascinated. *Is this guy for real?*

"A single drop of passion potion"—the strange shopkeeper's voice rose louder—"and ..." He squeezed the eyedropper. A churning drop of red liquid fell into the white fluid. The fluid began to rumble and crackle.

"Look out!" Sardo shouted, sounding less like a confident preacher and more like an inexperienced altar boy who'd just knocked over a candelabra. Sardo dove under the desk. Rush did the same, pulling the magic kit down with him.

A nine-foot plume of white flame jumped up from the caldron, throwing off sparks. It subsided and vanished, leaving thick billows of gray smoke. The white fluid bubbled over and dripped down the caldron onto the desk.

The shopkeeper raised his pudgy head and regarded the caldron with the suspicious curiosity of a scientist examining an odd and ugly species of bug. "Perhaps I added too much ginseng." He continued to study the white bubbles.

Rush smiled weakly at him. "Uh, I don't really need a love potion." He grabbed the magic box and headed toward the door.

Sardo uttered a strangled cry and scrambled after his customer. The man may not have understood his own merchandise, but he knew one thing: never let a wallet walk away until it's empty. He laid a heavy arm on Rush's shoulder. Rush sighed. *Am I gonna need a crowbar to get this guy away from me?*

In a pleading tone, the shopkeeper went on, "Surely there must be something I can interest you in." He looked across the store, his eyes bright. "Perhaps a flask of popularity potion!"

"No, thanks," said Rush. As Sardo glanced around the room to find something else to sell, Rush looked toward the door. "I gotta get home and—"

In an alcove behind the doorway, on a little table, stood a wooden chest. Decades of foul weather had left the chest dark and blemished. Bands of riveted black metal held its floor and walls together. Above the chest hung a bright, hand-lettered sign in the shape of a sunburst: OPEN THE CHEST! WIN A PRIZE!

"What's that?" Rush asked.

The shopkeeper scrunched up his face in disgust. "Oh, that. Forget it." He leaned toward Rush and took on the cocky, preaching tone again. "But I do have some wonderful crystals—"

"You get a prize just for opening it?" The chest didn't even have a lock. Without knowing why, Rush found himself compelled to stare at it.

"Don't waste your time!" Sardo squeaked. He shouldered past Rush and picked up a heavy hammer and chisel that lay next to the chest. "I tried everything." He pounded the chisel on the chest; it didn't budge. He dropped the tools onto the table. "It doesn't open!" A predatory grin spread over his lips, and the confident tone returned to his voice. "Now . . . have you seen our vomit?" He bustled toward a pile of boxes.

Rush ignored him. He couldn't stop looking at the chest. Why didn't it open?

And why couldn't he take his eyes away from it?

Rush had once watched a neighbor's cat stalk an unsuspecting blue jay. Although the cat was the predator, the jay seemed to have all the power. Its mere presence pulled the cat like a magnet, compelling the cat to follow its tiniest movements.

Rush felt like the cat. He couldn't stop himself from stepping toward the chest.

24

He laid his hand on the lid and pulled it up easily. Ancient dust and stale air swirled up from the darkness inside.

Rush's jaw fell. "Uh, Mr. Sardo?"

The shopkeeper stopped instantly. His shoulders tensed, and his hands formed fists. "That's Sar-DO!" He whirled to face Rush. "No 'mister,' accent on the—"

Sardo cut himself off. "You . . . you opened it!" He hurried over, his eyes wide as dinner plates, and joined Rush in staring into the chest. "I'm shocked. I'm amazed." He looked up and hissed. "I'm rich."

Rush looked up, distracted by Sardo's raw greed. "What's the big deal?" he asked.

"The man who gave me this chest," Sardo replied, his squeaky voice rising higher and louder with each excited word, "said if anyone could open it, he would give me five thousand dol—" He stopped and calmed himself. "Five thousand dolls." He added, much too quickly, "I'm a collector, you see." He glanced cautiously at Rush.

Yeah, sure, whatever, Rush thought. "So what do I get for opening it?"

The enthusiasm returned to Sardo's voice. "That's all part of the deal! Whoever opens it gets to keep what's in the chest." He reached in, careful not to touch the moldy cobwebs in a corner of the lid, and pulled out a dagger and a key. Something else rattled inside as well.

The key was longer than Sardo's hand, and old. Its black finish was flaking off, revealing the gray iron beneath. The handle was a circle, the teeth two long rectangles.

The dagger was a stumpy little thing. The black handle was as short as a teaspoon and thick as a garden hose, its surface braided in a crisscross pattern and encrusted with the dust of centuries. The blade, caked with grime, had gone dull and rusty over the decades. The whole thing was no bigger than an ordinary dinner knife.

"That's it?" Rush asked.

"Well, I didn't say it was a very good prize," said Sardo. He seemed disappointed himself.

"Rip. Keep it," Rush said. He turned toward the door.

"Wait!" Sardo screeched. He dropped the objects into the chest. "You have to take it!"

Reluctantly, Rush turned back. "But it's garbage!"

Rush reached into the chest and pulled out the third and last object: an old brown spyglass, built like a telescope with a small tube inside a bigger one. He pulled the spyglass open, raised it to one eye, and peered through the lens.

26

He saw a field of flat blackness, except for a very dim building in the distance. That was odd—there was no such building inside the Magic Mansion—but as far as Rush was concerned, it only proved his point.

"It's busted," he added in disgust. "What am I gonna do with a busted spyglass?"

CHAPTER 4

Mr. Sardo—Sar-DO, Rush corrected himself—was a lot more persuasive than he looked. Or maybe it was just that the tubby huckster wouldn't let Rush leave his shop without at least taking the spyglass (although Rush managed to escape without the dagger and key).

In any event, Rush found himself hours later looking through the spyglass again. The sight was the same: thick blackness and the faint, almost invisible building.

Rush stopped trying to make sense of the view and lowered the spyglass. He was standing in his own home, before the mirror in the foyer. He now wore his favorite shirt, the orange one that was so expensive he'd had to borrow money from Dad and even Max to buy it (and wasn't Mom angry at that!). His hair was shampooed until it shone, and combed until perfect.

He handed the spyglass to Max, who was, as usual, tagging along. "Here," Rush continued. "Maybe you can fix it."

"Cool!" Max exclaimed. "Thanks." He carefully raised the tube to his eye. Inside, he saw a surprising sight: the foyer, magnified in perfectly clear detail, from the sailing-ship model on the credenza to the painting of stormy seas on the wall. He then looked over at Rush, who was checking himself in the mirror and tucking in his shirt. "What do you mean?" Max asked. "It's not busted."

The doorbell rang. "Go away!" Rush commanded. He waved his brother off. Max ran to the living-room couch, where Rush had dumped the magic kit, and took the kit upstairs, grinning with anticipation.

Rush anxiously scanned the foyer: was everything in place? Had Max left that embarrassing toy sword lying around? He stepped toward the doorway and went back to the mirror to check his collar. *Okay,* he thought. *Perfect.* He scampered to the doorway, took a deep breath, and opened the door.

"Hi," said Sandy. She looked gorgeous. Her lustrous hair and porcelain skin glowed in the light of the front-porch lantern. She looked at Rush and smiled.

Max was smiling, too—at the magic kit under his arm. He entered the bedroom that he shared with Rush.

They each had a bed, chest of drawers, closet, desk, and window. Like the rest of the house, Max's side of the bedroom was decorated in sailor style. Posters showing ocean fish and seashore sunsets covered the walls. On the antique night table next to his bed stood a lamp with its switch embedded in a miniature ship's wheel. Throw rugs designed like seamen's maps lay on the hardwood floor. Above Max's bed hung framed drawings of old ships, as well as signal flags of the kind that flutter from sailboat masts.

Rush's side of the bedroom was different. He had rebelled against letting Mom and Dad's nautical tastes cover the room. Instead of fish and ships, his walls boasted posters of rock stars slamming guitars. Unlike Max's antique furniture, Rush's fixtures were new and streamlined. Compact discs stood stacked on his desk, next to his computer; a tennis racket hung on the wall by his bed.

Max thumped the spyglass down on the desk

30

blotter next to a model windjammer. Kneeling at the side of his bed, he placed the magic kit on the covers, and with a contented smile slid off the wooden lid and laid it against the side of the box. He pulled out a tiny jar of flash powder and a bottle of fake blood.

He heard something rattle behind him.

Max looked up and stopped pulling items from the chest. There was no one else in the room. There couldn't be anything moving.

The rattling continued. Whatever it was, it was getting louder.

Nothing in the room had ever made such a noise. What could it be? A practical joke by Rush? A burglar trying to sneak in through the window?

Max looked over his shoulder. A chill spread over him.

The spyglass was alive.

It twitched. It quivered. It vibrated and bounced, knocking fast and insistently against a book, hitting the book's hard cover like an intruder rapping on a door and demanding to be let inside.

With wary eyes, Max slowly approached the little brown tube. It continued to shake, drumming faster and louder. With every step that Max took, it got more excited. It wanted his attention.

31

But why?

And was it alive, or was someone controlling it?

Max stopped in front of the desk. The spyglass seemed to notice; it stopped knocking. Max froze. Had the spyglass stopped for good, or was it preparing to do something even more bizarre?

Very carefully, Max reached toward the tube. As his fingers were about to make contact, the tube began to spin in place atop the book.

In the living room, Rush and Sandy were sitting on the couch. Not talking or touching or kissing, just sitting.

What should I say? Rush wondered. He and Sandy looked at the couch, their laps, and their own hands, as if those things would tell them how to create a sparkling evening. The awkward silence between them stretched on and on.

Suddenly, Rush spoke. "I'm really glad you came over tonight."

"Me, too," Sandy agreed with a smile. She looked away.

Well, that didn't work, Rush thought. He tried another idea. "You want something to eat?"

"No, thanks," Sandy answered—but at least now she was looking at him. *Now, what do I do?* Rush wondered. They both glanced away.

Rush drummed his fingers on his pants. He

32

wanted his arms around the girl—but how? What would get her interested?

He turned back to Sandy. "My parents are on a bike trip all weekend." He added with slow emphasis, "Far, far away."

"Yeah," Sandy said. "You told me."

Rush looked away. *I am so lame!* Again the silence stretched out before them. Sandy waited for him to reply. She seemed bored, even exasperated. *Do something!* he thought to himself.

An idea struck him. He turned to Sandy. All in one fast breath, he announced, "I don't suppose there's any chance we could make out?" He let out a nervous, little laugh.

So did Sandy. It was the tiniest giggle through closed lips, but it was there, and the lips were smiling. Rush laughed again. For the first time, he breathed easily.

The two teenagers stared silently at each other. They leaned in close, and Sandy shut her eyes. Their bodies and faces drew near, ready to touch.

"This thing is weird!"

Rush and Sandy jumped part. Max, behind the couch, shoved the spyglass between their faces.

Rush closed his eyes and wished Max dead. When he opened them an instant later, Max was bending over the back of the couch, peering into the spyglass. Rush took slow, deep breaths to calm his anger.

33

Max brought the spyglass down from his eye. "It was moving by itself." He sounded amazed.

"Don't be strange," Rush ordered. He grabbed the spyglass from Max's hand and looked into it. He saw the same flat blackness that he had seen before, but in front of it stood fuzzy gray blobs. Some looked like crosses; others, like upside-down letter U's. In the distance sat a blurred version of the dim building that Rush had seen earlier. Max, Rush decided, must have jammed some pieces of the spyglass loose.

Good going, wormboy, Rush thought. *Thanks for showing Sandy I've got a nutbar for a brother. You better not embarrass me any more.*

"Were you guys gonna kiss?" Max asked.

Arrrgh!

Upstairs, a white fog gathered outside Max's bedroom window. It grew and swelled, filling the panes, and blew the glass open. The fog burst into the room like an explosion.

Someone sinister floated inside the fog, piloting it like a ship.

The unholy being banished the fog; it floated through the window and out of sight. The intruder prowled the room, exploring the shadows under the bed and examining the closets.

He selected a place to hide and waited. . . .

34

*   *   *

In the living room, Rush was getting tired of his brother's wild ideas. "I'm telling you, it's busted," Rush insisted, lowering the spyglass.

"It's not!" Max whined. "It was spinning around, I swear."

Rush sighed. *Can't you see that I'm busy?* "Look," he said patiently, "I'll make you a deal." He looked his brother in the eye, smiled, and went on gently, as if talking to a baby. "You go upstairs . . . you leave us alone . . . and I won't make you *eat* this!" He thrust the spyglass at Max's face. "How's that?" Rush finished, shifting to a threatening glare.

Max took the spyglass. "That's a good deal," he said hastily. "G'night." He clambered upstairs to the bedroom.

" 'Night, Max," Sandy called. She settled back on the couch and smiled warmly at Rush. "He's cute," she said.

"A teddy bear is cute," Rush grumbled. "Max is a festering sore." He blinked and remembered why he and Sandy were there. "Now," he went on in his most sophisticated tone, "where were we?" He leaned toward Sandy, his lips ready for hers.

"Maybe I am hungry," Sandy said. She launched herself up from the couch and headed

35

for the kitchen. Rush fell facedown onto the cushion where Sandy had been sitting. He pounded the cushion quietly. *Max, you die for this.*

Max trudged into the bedroom. He knew that he shouldn't have interrupted Rush and Sandy, but Rush shouldn't have thrown him out, either. *All I wanted was to show him something interesting. It's not fair.*

Max did not notice the hidden intruder.

But the intruder noticed him. The intruder smiled and prepared to strike.

Max looked at the spyglass in his hands, determined to give Rush proof that it really was doing something weird. He was about to place the spyglass back on his diary, to see if it would start twitching and spinning again, when a cold breeze brushed his cheek.

He turned in the direction of the breeze. To his surprise, the bedroom windows were open. He could have sworn that they were shut when he was last in the room.

Max laid the spyglass on the desk, stepped over and closed the windows.

His closet door slammed.

Max turned. He knew for certain that he'd left the closet closed. Someone must be in there. Someone had come in the window and was hiding in the closet.

36

Get Rush! he thought—but no; Rush would be too angry to listen. Max had to handle the mystery alone.

Very slowly, he walked over to the closet, trying to keep his footsteps silent on the hardwood floor. The intruder waited, ready to attack, as Max drew closer and closer.

Max approached the door. He stared at its glass knob, not wanting to touch it but knowing that he had to. He reached for it and yanked the door open, forcing himself to face whatever lurked inside.

He saw his own clothes.

There was nothing unusual in the closet. Max slumped. The sight only made things worse.

Whoever had shut the door wasn't hiding in the closet; he must have escaped the closet. He must be somewhere in the house.

I gotta find him! Max thought. He turned around.

Someone was behind him.

"What is your problem?" Rush asked.

He was standing behind Max, riffling through some compact discs on his desk. He glanced up at Max with distaste, as if his brother were a plate of particularly rancid spinach, and turned back to his task.

"Why're you sneaking up on me?" Max demanded.

"I'm not." *Crazy kid,* Rush thought. "I'm just getting some CDs." Rush picked up the discs, threw Max an annoyed glance, and left.

Max watched him go. He was facing bizarre dangers, he was clearly scared witless, and his big brother didn't care. Feeling hurt, Max plopped down heavily onto his bed. He idly picked up a foam ball from the magic kit.

A low rumble came from his desk. The spyglass was rolling back and forth on the mahogany surface.

Max stared. The hairs on his arms stood up, and goose pimples rose up from his skin. The spyglass kept rolling, tempting Max to come closer.

Never letting his eyes leave the spyglass, he carefully approached the desk.

The intruder, in his hiding place, watched Max's nervous face with quiet glee.

With rising fear, Max called, "Rush?"

The spyglass whirled across the desk and leaped off the table, smacking the hardwood floor.

Stop it, Max thought. *You're driving me nuts!*

The spyglass rolled over a throw rug and traveled toward Max's bed.

This can't be happening, Max thought. *I wish Rush was here. I wish Mom was here. I've gotta get outta here!*

But he couldn't stop watching the tube as it made its slow way forward.

The little telescope stopped on a rug at the foot of Max's bed, waiting. *That's it, I've had enough!* He kneeled and reached for the spyglass.

The bedroom door slammed. Max turned to see who had closed it, but no one was there. He gazed at the door, his hands dangling in midair.

The intruder grabbed him.

CHAPTER 5

Rush was sitting on the living-room couch, holding the compact discs in his lap. He and Sandy were looking deep into each other's eyes. Neither of them moved.

"So," Rush began softly, "you wanna listen to some music, or . . . do you wanna . . ."

Sandy bent her head toward Rush. She reached out, wrapped her warm fingers around his shoulder, and touched her lips to his.

Rush dropped the CDs and devoted himself to Sandy. His arms wrapped around the girl; his hand slid through her long thick hair.

"Rush!" came a scream from the bedroom. "Help! Help, Rush!"

The teenagers jumped apart. "Aw, now what?" roared Rush, looking upstairs. He pulled his hands off of Sandy, shot up from the couch, and headed for the stairs. *If that little bug's pulling some trick . . .*

"I'd better go," Sandy said, out of breath. She ran her fingers through her rumpled hair, smoothing it out.

Rush turned back and reached out to stop her. "No, no, no," he insisted. "I'll be right back." He headed for the stairs, leaving Sandy dazed.

Reaching out from the cold darkness under the bed, the intruder's gloved hand surrounded Max's thin wrist and hauled him forward. *He was here!* Max realized. *He was here all the time!*

Max tried to pull away, but the hand was too strong. As he screamed, the intruder laughed: a raspy dry cackle.

Max yanked free and fell backward, landing hard on the rug. He looked at his wrist; the intruder's gauntlet still held it tight. Max had pulled the glove, a large brown leather antique, clean off the intruder's hand.

From under the bed, the hand grabbed his ankle. Max gasped.

The hand had no skin.

It was the bony hand of a living skeleton. The

41

hard strong fingers pressed into his flesh and yanked him forward.

Max jammed his feet against the throw rugs to brake his slide, but the rugs buckled and slipped on the slick floor. The intruder yanked again, and Max's feet slid under the bed. He tried to kick free, but something felt wrong. He glanced down under the bed and saw his feet dissolving into nothingness.

Max clutched at the floor, but its polished surface was too smooth to grip. Cold air whistled up his calves as they slid into the darkness. He could feel them dissolving.

Get me out of this! Somebody, please, get me out of this!

He scrambled and pushed and fought, but kept sliding uncontrollably toward the grasping, powerful thing in the darkness. His knees banged against the bottom of the bed, but the intruder wrapped bony arms around them and dragged them under. They disappeared. The bony fingers clutched his hips and kept pulling.

From the chilly darkness, Max heard a rough crackling voice. "Give it up, lad." It had a wheezy English accent and a teasing, smug lilt. "Come with me." The hem of the bedspread brushed Max's shirt as the skeletal thing pulled him forward.

Writhing helplessly, Max screamed. "Help, Rush! *Help!*"

"What is your problem?" Rush shouted. He marched through the doorway, furious.

Max's legs and feet instantly reappeared. He pulled himself out from under the bed and scrambled to his feet, picking up the spyglass from the floor. "Oh, man, Rush," he whimpered, "there's a skeleton. It was dragging me under the bed!" Trembling, Max grabbed his brother's shoulder and pushed him toward the bed. "Look. Look!"

Now what's the little zit trying to pull? Rush wondered. He pushed the hem of the covers to the top of the bed and kneeled down, his head almost touching the floor. He looked back at Max for a moment—*You better not be lying*—and peered under the bed.

Nothing was there but dust and one of Max's sneakers. Rush shoved the bedspread back down and stalked past Max angrily. "You're not gonna get me. No way!" He stalked out the door and slammed it behind him.

Max opened the door, glanced back at the bed, and hurried after his brother. He scrambled down the stairs, still carrying the spyglass. "I'm not lying," he wailed. "It was a skeleton! It must've come in through the window!"

Rush kept moving. He had always hated that

painful, wailing tone. He'd heard it for years; Max used it to insist on his honesty whenever people doubted him.

Rush stopped at the living-room couch—the empty living-room couch. No one was in sight.

"Oh, man." He sighed. "Sandy!" He stared, frustrated, at the spot where the two of them had been kissing. *Thanks, Max. One weekend to run my own life, and you blow it.*

Max's shrill cry cut through the air. "We gotta call the cops or some—"

Rush spun and glowered. "Look, you little snot. I'm tired of you messing things up all the time!"

Max was frantic. "But the spyglass—"

"I don't care!" Rush shouted, every word like a fist in his brother's face. "I don't care about your stories. I don't care about your problems. I don't care about you! Get out of my life!"

Max looked as if he were about to crumble. Rush couldn't stand to look at him.

His gaze dropped to Max's hand and the spyglass. *If Max wasn't playing with that stupid telescope, Sandy'd still be here!* Rush ripped the tube from Max's fingers and pounded up the stairs.

Max didn't know whether to yell, fight, or cry. He'd never seen Rush so angry. He knew that Rush wasn't being fair. But Max knew better than to go up and argue with him. Rush would just yell again.

Besides, the thing under the bed might still be up there.

Outside, thunder cracked and boomed. A storm was boiling up.

Scanning the room for trouble, Max lay down on the couch, pulled off the coverlet, and wrapped it around himself for protection. Filled with dread, he continued to watch the room as if the familiar walls had become a jungle hiding a ravenous, crouching tiger.

Upstairs, Rush sat down heavily on the edge of his bed, holding the spyglass in both hands. *I oughtta throw this thing out the window.* He sighed. *Naw, that'd just make Max even nuttier than he is. What's so important about the stupid thing anyhow?* He pulled out the inside tube, extending the telescope to its full length, and raised it to his eye.

Fuzzy gray shapes floated against the black background, just as they had before. Rush snapped the spyglass shut and stood it on the night table next to his bed. "Great weekend," he grunted.

He lay down on his bed, clasped his hands over his stomach, and stared at the ceiling.

Where am I?
Rush stood between a tall hedge and the black

45

pedestal of an even taller statue. He stepped forward, finding himself outside in the cold, misty night air, walking on dewy grass. Moonlight shone down onto dozens of nearby knee-high tombstones.

What am I doing in a cemetery? How'd I get here?

He did not see that a white fog—the same one that had entered the bedroom—was following behind him. Inside the fog sat the bedroom intruder.

Rush could feel someone watching him. "Hello?" he asked.

The intruder laughed at him. Someone else laughed as well—a low, guttural laugh.

Rush looked around, but no one was there. To sound tough and unafraid, he went on in a challenging tone, "Who's there?"

Rush stepped past knee-high tombstones, searching for the source of the laughter. *What's so funny? Who's watching me?*

He heard another laugh. It was coming from directly ahead of him.

Before him stood the biggest object in the cemetery: an ancient two-story building built from thick stone bricks. Its black door stood fifteen feet tall, flanked by square columns thicker than telephone poles. Taller than the surrounding trees, the building dominated other monuments

46

like a mountain looming over a lowland village.

It was a mausoleum, a giant tomb, and the only place to find someone who could answer Rush's questions.

Rush's throat went dry. He swallowed, took a deep breath, and forced himself to step forward. Who would hide inside a building full of dead bodies?

And what would happen if Rush tried to break in?

Slow minutes later, he reached the doorway. The deep rough voice laughed at him again. *This is nuts,* Rush thought. *Those people won't help me. I'm not going in there!* Backing away a few paces, he turned to leave the cemetery.

A ghostly man with a slit throat stood staring at him with wide, pale blue eyes.

The man's scar traced a bloody line against the chalky paleness of his skin. Dark circles underneath his wild staring eyes gave him the look of a whipped animal. Rank, stringy hair hung below his shoulders. He was soiled and grimy, as if he had just crawled out of a grave.

On his gaunt body hung the clothes of an old-time seaman. His dirty white shirt had billowing, blousy sleeves; he wore not a belt but a white sash; his snowy sailcloth pants hung loose and shapeless.

47

The man, pale all over, floated a few inches above the grass. He stood still as death, silently staring with the anxious face of a prisoner begging a judge to let him free. Rush gulped.

"It is you," the man said. "You're the one."

Rush backed away. *A ghost. This can't be happening. There's no such thing as ghosts!*

Rush tried to speak. "Who are you?"

"What he wants is not what he desires," said the ghost, with great urgency. He had an Irish accent and seemed to be in a terrible hurry.

"What?" Rush didn't get it. He continued to back off.

The man noticed Rush's anxiety. He spoke more slowly now, and more calmly. "What he wants is not what he desires," he repeated. "Do not be fool—"

The mausoleum door moved.

Rush and the ghost looked up. Behind Rush, the door banged and rattled and creaked. Someone was shaking it open.

The ghost gasped. "Remember me words!" he cried, and disappeared.

No! Rush thought. *Don't leave me alone!* He ran toward the spot where the ghost had stood. But there was no bringing the ghost back; Rush was alone, and a thing that could terrify the undead was about to burst free.

Something rough and strong slithered over his feet.

Rush looked down and gasped. Woody vines from the grass whipped around his ankles and calves. They slithered up his pants like octopus tentacles, binding his knees and crawling up his thighs. They squeezed his legs like long scratchy claws.

Rush could hear the door stop creaking. It was wide open now. The being inside was free—and coming for Rush. He could hear heavy boots crunching on the mausoleum's stone threshold.

Get away from me! Rush thought. He tried to run, but the gnarled vines were wound too tight. There was no way out.

"I've been waitin' for the battle, lad," came a rough, guttural voice, getting closer with every step.

What battle? Rush thought. *I can't fight a battle!*

Over Rush's shoulder slid a skeletal hand wearing a giant blue sapphire ring. The voice came closer. "Are you a match for me?" The bony index finger reached for Rush's cheek.

Rush screamed.

CHAPTER 6

Rush woke up, panting and sweaty in bed. Morning sunlight streamed in through the window.

He sat up, still panting. *A dream,* he thought, *just a dream.*

He pulled himself out from under the covers and sat upright. The quick move made him dizzy; he nearly fell backward. To steady himself, he grabbed the covers, gulped a lungful of air, and blinked in the sunlight.

His eyes landed on the spyglass, standing where he'd left it on the night table. *That thing did something to me!* He looked away. *No. Can't be. It's just a piece of metal and glass, and it's busted!*

50

Rush made himself pick up the old brown cylinder. He pulled out the interior tube and raised the spyglass to his eyes.

He could now see clearly the fuzzy U's and crosses that had appeared through the glass earlier. They were the tombstones that he had passed while walking in the dream.

"What?" *That's impossible!*

He looked through the glass again. The mausoleum came into view, and he saw himself walking toward it.

Rush gaped at the little telescope, panting with fear. Then he burst out of the room like a cannonball, glancing, as he passed the bedroom door, at a note taped there:

I'm at Tony's. I'll be there all day. It's too weird around here.

Max

"Mr. Sardo?" Rush cried. Still clutching the spyglass, he marched into the Magic Mansion. "Mr. Sardo!"

"That's Sar-DO!" The indignant shout boomed out from behind a green velvet curtain near the desk where the silver caldron had bubbled over.

The pudgy shopkeeper swept aside the curtain. Apparently, a room lay back there. The drape

51

swung into place behind him. He smiled and went on lightly, almost singing, "No 'mister,' accent on the 'do,' " his fingers darting through the air as if pointing at an invisible blackboard.

Rush shook his head. *This loon is going to tell me what's up with this spyglass? Boy, am I in trouble.*

Sardo pointed at Rush. "You!" Sardo hooted, recognizing him. Giddy with delight, he went on, "You're back!" The shopkeeper giggled gleefully and twiddled his fingers. "Perfect!"

He crossed over to his desk. The silver caldron was gone. In its place stood the wooden chest that Rush had opened. Sardo put his hands gently on the old box as if it were the world's most delicate, valuable rarity. "Now, kindly take the rest of this stuff so I can collect my—"

"No!" Rush declared. He strode over to the table and slammed the spyglass onto it. "Keep it. I don't want it." He turned and headed out the door, glad to be rid of the annoying tube.

"Wait!" Sardo cried shrilly. He bounded around the table and waddled after Rush. "What about my five thousand—"

"Let him go!" a deep voice commanded.

Sardo stopped. A man in a heavy jacket and dark cloak emerged from behind the curtain.

The shopkeeper was confused. "But you said he had to take all of the—"

52

"Please," said the stranger, weary at Sardo's short-sightedness. He approached the spyglass. "The items belong to him now," he explained patiently. "He's just not ready to accept them."

The man swept his cloak over the spyglass. When he lowered it a second later, the spyglass was gone. Sardo approached the cloaked man, staring in amazement at the spot where the old cylinder had once stood.

With serene assurance, the stranger went on, "The boy will be back." He reached into a pocket and pulled out a roll of hundred-dollar bills. Sardo focused on them as if they were tender strips of bacon and he had spent the last month fasting.

The cloaked man added, "And when he returns, send him"—he waved the roll before Sardo's eyes—"to me."

Sardo, entranced, reached slowly for the bills. The stranger snatched them back.

The shopkeeper grinned weakly. As he watched the money return to the stranger's pocket, his smile faded, and he wondered what kind of trouble he had gotten himself into.

Down the block from the Magic Mansion, Rush found a pay phone. He called Sandy, but reached only an answering machine. After leaving an apology for the previous night, he spent the rest of the day wandering from movie theater to hot-dog

53

stand to video arcade, trying to take his mind off the spyglass.

Hours passed. A cold night fell. The air was still. The only noise near the Keegan house came from the water of Prospect Sound as it lapped against the nearby shore.

Max cracked his bedroom door open and stuck his head in, peeking from right to left. "Hello?" he ventured.

He had been with Tony since breakfast, telling him all about the skeleton, and had hoped to stay overnight at Tony's home to keep away from it. Tony's mother objected. Max's wild stories, she felt, were getting Tony all wound up. She drove Max home and pulled away as he closed the front door behind him.

Alone in the house, Max felt restless. He decided to retrieve the magic kit.

But what if the skeleton was still up there?

On the other hand, maybe it wasn't. It had, after all, vanished last night. Maybe it was gone for good.

There was only one way to find out. Max peered into the silent bedroom. It seemed normal; no strange noises, no mysterious movements. With nervous eyes, he glanced around at the floor. No skeletal hands, no rolling spyglasses.

54

The magic set lay on the bedspread where he had left it. He carefully made his way toward the bed. *Just get the kit and get out of here,* he told himself. *It's easy. Get the kit and get out.*

Something punched the windows open. They slammed against the wall, thrown back by a hurricane-force wind blast. The gust hit Max in the face like a baseball bat. He dove behind the bed and hid, shivering.

He raised his head slowly. The wind was gone. *What's going on here?* He went to the window, staring at the inky night and the branches of nearby trees, searching for answers.

A mournful, alluring sea chantey rolled in.

A dull stupor stole over Max. He no longer felt afraid. Hypnotized by the music, he turned from the window and slowly left the bedroom, following the song to its source. At a steady pace, he walked out the front door, across the front lawn, and toward the lake. He stopped by a tree stump near the shore.

On the stump lay the spyglass.

Max took the spyglass from the stump and looked at it idly. He vaguely recognized the little tube, but it didn't matter to him anymore.

Oars splashed through the water. As the splashing noise grew louder and nearer, Max looked up to see the white fog rolling over the lake and heading his way.

A small rowboat paddled out of the fog. At the back of the boat, a white lantern swung from a pole. In the front, with his back to Max, a man rowed wooden oars that had gone gray with age. He wore colonial-era foul-weather gear that looked like a hooded raincoat of rough canvas.

The music was louder now, and it came from the man. Although he played no instrument, the music flowed from him like an aroma. It swam around Max, muffling his thoughts and wrapping him in an embrace that held him perfectly still. Within the boat, the oarsman grinned.

Rush pushed the front door open and entered the foyer.

He had had enough. No matter how hard he'd tried, Rush couldn't ignore the weirdness and worry that the spyglass had brought on. He needed answers, and that meant Max. Max was the only one who knew about the telescope, except for Sardo, and Sardo's shop was closed.

"Max?" Rush shouted. No answer. He glanced around the foyer. "Max!"

The front door slammed behind him.

Rush spun and stared at it, shocked. He had lived in that house all of his life, and the door had never shut by itself. *It's all getting worse,* he thought. *Find Max!*

56

Rush climbed the stairs. "Max?" He entered their bedroom and looked around. There was no one in the room. "Where are you, you little—"

Something rapped on Max's closet door.

Rush froze. *Someone's in there!*

Slowly, quietly, he moved toward the closet. Anyone could be in there. A burglar. A kidnapper.

Or something worse.

Taking a deep breath, Rush stared at the crystal doorknob and took another step. Whoever was lurking behind the door probably didn't want witnesses. If anyone saw him, he would be angry. He would be furious.

Even murderous.

His fingers inches from the doorknob, Rush wondered who or what was inside. What would it do if he opened the door. Would it leap out and attack?

Gotta be ready. Gotta fight him. Yeah. Of course. I can do it. I know I can.

God, don't let him hurt me!

He yanked the knob.

He saw Max's clothes swaying gently on their hangers and nothing else. Rush cautiously reached between the shirts and sweaters to feel for anything that might have knocked on the door.

Nothing unusual was there. Maybe the wind had seeped in and knocked a hanger into the door.

Rush was disgusted. *Max, this is your fault. All that noise about skeletons—you got me spooked for nothing.* He turned back into the bedroom.

He caught something strange out of the corner of his eye.

Slowly, he turned. A page of curling yellow parchment hung inside the closet door. Someone had stabbed an ancient knife through the paper, pinning it to the wood.

On the parchment, in old-fashioned Gothic script, Rush read the following:

> This is no dream
> The boy is mine

CHAPTER 7

Rush backed away. He turned and galloped out of the room.

"Max?" Rush bolted down the stairs and into the foyer. "Max!" He stopped and looked around. "C'mon, Max, answer me!"

No reply. Max was gone.

A faint splashing noise cut through the silence. Rush raced to the windows and pushed the curtains aside. Through the glass, across the dark lawn, he saw a small, familiar figure standing by a tree stump.

Max! Rush shot out the front door into the icy night.

He skidded to a stop next to his brother, panting. Max stood by the stump on the lake shore, holding the spyglass. As still as a statue, Max gazed at the lake with blank eyes, mesmerized by the approach of the rowboat.

Rush grabbed Max's arm and shouted, "What're you doing?" Why was Max standing out in the middle of the night in the freezing cold, staring at the water? Was Max nuts?

He noticed the spyglass in Max's hands. *I got rid of that thing. It can't be here!* A chill ran down his back. *What is going on?*

With smooth, even strokes, the man in the boat pulled toward the shore. The boat closed in on the brothers, its lantern swinging with every swish of the oars, and bumped the shore.

The boat's prow lodged in the sandy lake bottom. The man in the hooded jacket laid the oars down inside the boat and waited as Max continued to stare.

You, Rush thought. Rush felt his heart drumming hard, punching his chest. *You're making this happen. Well, it stops now!*

Rush headed for the boat and took a deep breath. "My father's gonna be here any second."

The man in the boat said nothing, nor did he move. *Answer me, you creep!* Rush thought. "Look, pal ..." he began. He grabbed the man's shoulder, spinning him around and sending his hood flying.

60

Under the hood was a skull. A skeleton was rowing the boat—the skeleton that had attacked Max! Rush stumbled back. As he watched in open-mouthed amazement and horror, the skeleton underwent a remarkable transformation. With a wet crackle, like bacon frying, flesh flowed onto the bones.

As Rush gaped, the skeleton became a man, heavily tanned from seafaring years under the glaring sun. A thick flap of skin lay over one eye like a patch. A fringe of rough beard covered his chin. His scraggly hair was a dull black from years without a wash.

But the worst part was his grinning mouth. The cracked, burned lips surrounded teeth, stained brown and yellow, that leaned against each other like weather-beaten fence posts—except for the three front teeth. The man didn't have them.

Rush backed away, swallowing hard.

The man rose and grinned wider. He shook his head at Rush. In a wheezy English accent with a teasing, smug lilt, he crooned, "Your father ain't here ..." Suddenly, the man turned furious, and his singsong tone became a harsh growl. "... and I've come for the boy!" He let out a breathy laugh, rough as sandpaper, and leered at Rush, flexing his fingers as if crushing a small animal.

61

Rush bolted. Looking over his shoulder as he ran, he grabbed Max's arm. It felt as limp as wet spaghetti. Max dropped the spyglass and passively followed his brother.

Rush barreled toward the house and shoved the front door open. He pulled Max inside. "C'mon. We gotta call the cops." Rush grabbed his brother by the shoulders and pushed him toward the living room.

The rowboat man leaped into the hallway ahead of them.

He was quick and springy for someone so decrepit. As Rush stared, the man giggled—a harsh, scratchy noise. "No use in running," he rasped. "We got ya now!" With mad glee, he cackled, stretching gnarled, clawlike hands toward the boys.

Rush pushed Max back to the front door. *We're getting out of here!*

The doorknob rattled. Rush froze.

A powerful blow broke the door open, and a blast of light flooded the foyer. Blinded, Rush blinked and squinted into the glare.

As his vision began to clear, he saw a gigantic man fill the doorway. The man lumbered toward Rush and Max like a grizzly bear, his boots landing heavily on the foyer's hardwood floor.

62

The man wore a long, bulky, navy-blue military greatcoat with fringed shoulder epaulets and silver trim. A black bandoleer ran around his neck and down to his waist, where it held a long saber.

The man's head was bald as a rock and enormous. A gold ring hung from one ear. His face was full and strong. Scarred skin partly covered an eye. On his powerful right hand, he wore a giant blue sapphire ring, exactly like the one on the skeletal hand in Rush's nightmare. The man was an angry mountain, a thundering storm cloud.

And he was glaring at Rush.

Rush gaped at him. He didn't know what to do.

The man spoke. His voice was deep, rough, and guttural—the laughing voice from the mausoleum in Rush's dream, the voice of the skeleton wearing the blue sapphire. "Did ya really think you had a chance against me, skipper?" He smiled.

Rush put an arm on Max's chest and pushed him back, away from the monstrous giant before them. Max, still in a daze, watched the man.

Inside, Rush was screaming. *What do I say? What do I do?* He forced out a few words. "Who—who are you?" His voice shook.

"Mr. Noise!" the man shouted, looking over Rush's head.

63

The rowboat sailor popped up behind Rush and Max. Growling like an angry dog, he wrapped an arm tightly around Rush's shoulders and throat. Rush gagged; he could smell the man's rank, bitter sweat. Max, standing next to them, did not react.

The big man stepped forward and bent down, pushing his vicious smirk toward Rush's face. As Rush shrunk back, the giant leaned in closer, his breath foul and hot on Rush's skin. Rush flinched.

"After all these years, you're nothing more than a young pup." The man chuckled. He seemed amused at the sight of someone so small and inexperienced. "So be it, then." To Rush's relief, the grinning man pulled away and stood in the blazing light streaming through the doorway. "Ahhh, look sharp, lad," he warned.

Mr. Noise, his arm still holding Rush, nudged Max forward. The boy stepped toward the colossus in the blue uniform. Rush reached out, but Mr. Noise held him back.

"Max?" Rush called.

Max kept going, still mesmerized. The giant laid a hand on the boy's shoulder.

"Leave my brother alone!" Rush shouted in agony. He stared at Max in despair. He looked so frail and helpless.

Smiling more widely, the big man slipped his massive hands under Max's armpits and hoisted him up effortlessly. He held the boy out toward Rush.

"Take a good look, skipper," the giant said. "It'll be for the last time." He chuckled again and tucked Max under his arm as if the boy were a loaf of bread.

The shock of being manhandled so roughly cracked Max's spell for a moment. He looked at his brother, full of longing and pain.

Save me, Rush!

Rush tried to reach for him. He writhed and struggled, but Mr. Noise held him tight.

The big man turned. Screeching with laughter, he carried Max out the door and into the light. The door slammed behind him.

Rush's arms dropped free. He looked behind him; Mr. Noise had vanished.

Rush's thoughts whirled in remorseful confusion. *It's my fault that Max—if I had only believed him . . .*

I'm coming, Max!

Rush sprinted out to the lake. He saw the rowboat out on the water, far from shore and moving out farther. Max sat motionless in the front of the boat, with Mr. Noise rowing in the middle and the big man standing in the back.

65

The giant waved an arm at Rush in a gesture of grand triumph.

No, Rush thought. *You can't do this!*

"You should have known, skipper," he bellowed. He jabbed a meaty thumb at his chest. "I always win, because I make up the rules!" He filled the night air with screaming rolls of laughter.

"Max!" Rush cried. *Max, do something!*

The boy remained still.

A massive cloud of white fog floated toward the boat. Mr. Noise rowed toward it, and the fog enveloped the little craft. It disappeared silently into the vast, opaque haze.

"Max!" Rush bolted into the lake, but the men and the rowboat had gone. Even the laughter had stopped.

Rush stood in the cold water, helpless. *What have I done? Max told me something was wrong . . . and all I could do was think about myself. Oh, Max . . . It's all my fault!* He turned back, looking for a clue that would help him free his brother. *What am I going to do?*

And then he saw it. On the sand nearby was the spyglass, lying where Max had dropped it. Breathing heavily, Rush slowly picked the spyglass up and raised the tube to his eyes. *C'mon, spyglass, show me where they're going!*

66

Again, he saw the mausoleum, but this time its door was open. Mr. Noise's white fog and the giant's white light were entering the doorway.

The door slammed. The fog and the light were gone, locked away and unreachable within the mausoleum's solid stone walls.

Clutching the spyglass, Rush ran into the night.

CHAPTER
8

Rush looked in the window of the Magic Mansion. Nothing moved inside the darkened shop. He dashed to the door.

Over the glass pane set in the door hung a circular sign displaying a closed and apparently sleeping eye. The word SORRY was lettered underneath. The shop was closed.

"Mr. Sardo?" he shouted. "Mr. Sardo, you in there?" He banged on the door. *Come on, be in there!* "Mr. Sardo, open up!"

"Sar-DO, Sar-DO!" shouted a whiny voice. "Oh, this is hopeless." A plump hand swept aside the curtain covering the shop's back room, and Sardo bustled out. Apparently, he slept there.

Sardo flipped on a light switch; several lamps turned on at once. He wrapped a belt around a satin smoking jacket that covered his silk pajamas.

"Go away," he ordered, shuffling past boxes and vials on his way to the door. "We're closed until—" He recognized Rush through the glass. "You!" He flipped the door sign; its backside showed an open eye and the word WELCOME. Unlocking the front door, the shopkeeper trilled, "I knew you'd be back." He seemed delighted.

Rush flung the door open. He pointed the spyglass at Sardo's nose. "Look, buddy," he declared, thrusting the tube closer, "I don't know what this thing is, but it's making ghosts show up at my house." He stalked forward, marching Sardo backward.

"Ghosts!" Sardo's voice rose to a frightened squeak. "Uh, yes, well, they're probably just illusions." He bumped into an exotic lamp.

"Yeah? Then two *illusions* just snatched my little brother." With cold determination, Rush forced Sardo back into a wall. "Either you tell me what's going on, or I'm coming back with the cops." He pushed the spyglass under Sardo's chin and pressed up.

Sardo's eyes narrowed. His expression turned skeptical. In a slow, silky tone, he murmured, "I'm not so sure the police would believe you any more than I do."

69

Rush lowered the spyglass. His shoulders drooped. "They don't," he muttered. "I've already tried." Sardo gazed down at him in haughty superiority.

Rush looked up, his eyes pleading. "Look, Mr. Sar—" Sardo leaned forward and raised a cautioning finger. Rush sighed again, wearily. "I mean 'Sar-DO.' " The man smiled and settled back, satisfied. In his most earnest tone, Rush went on, "All I want is my brother back."

Sardo shook his head. "I'm afraid I don't know much more than you." He thought for a moment. A sneaky grin slid across his face. "But there's someone who does," he whispered. He rummaged in the pockets of his jacket and pajamas, and then raised a white business card to Rush's eyes. Clearly, he kept it with him at all times.

The card featured a barber pole and the following words:

"WILD BOAR COIFFURE.
OPEN 24 HOURS.
110½ PROSPECT STREET."

"The Wild Boar Coiffure?" Rush asked. Confused, he plucked the card from Sardo's hand and studied it. "A barber shop?" He shot the chubby man a quizzical look.

70

"It's run by the same man who gave me the chest," Sardo explained. "I suggest you go and talk to him." He pointed a thick finger at the card and nodded with a sly smile. Rush looked at the card and turned to leave.

"Oh, uh . . ." Sardo called.

He sounded worried. Rush turned back to him. *Now what?*

"Don't be alarmed, but the fellow is a bit of a . . . oh, a . . ." He looked down for a moment, searching for the word. "A nutbag," he finished, full of disdain.

And he's my only choice, Rush thought.

Prospect Street had always been considered a jinx. It had started as the bed of the Prospect River, which drained off of Prospect Sound. In 1868, after heavy rains turned the river into a flood, the city council dammed the river, drained its bed, paved its bottom, and christened the new alley Prospect Street.

The alley lay twenty feet below the rest of the town, like a trench. The former riverbed still smelled of rotting moss and dead fish. Strange, decrepit shops lined the street. Most townspeople avoided it.

Except for a bag lady wearing ratty, fingerless gloves and warming her hands over a leaping fire in a trash can, Prospect Street was deserted. Rush, still holding the spyglass, paced carefully down the alley, looking from side to side for number 110½.

He poked his head into a deep shadowy corridor on one side of the alley, leading to a door as dark as tar. *Is this it?*

A guard dog on a chain leaped toward him, barking and snarling.

Rush backed away toward the opposite side of the alley. Something felt odd there, even odder than the rest of the street.

He turned. On the wall behind him hung iron numbers: 110½.

The building's blank stone front looked like no barber shop he'd ever seen. It had no window or sign or even a barber pole.

It did have a door, built of black steel. The door had once featured a glass plate like the door of Sardo's store, inviting potential customers to look inside, but the owner of the barbershop had covered the glass with a metal sheet. Whoever was inside must have secrets to hide. Rush frowned at the thought.

The door opened.

Out stepped a tall thin man neatly dressed in a conservative gray suit, white shirt, and black tie. His hair stood up, frizzy and bedraggled—odd for

72

a man who'd presumably just been to the barber. He stared at Rush, amused.

This can't be the right place, Rush thought. "Uh, is this the, uh"—he looked down at the card again—"Wild Boar?"

The man leaned back for a moment with a soulful stare. Then he let out a bubbling squeal of laughter and clapped his hands. With a hysterical screech, he raked the top of his head with his fingernails, like a chimpanzee. Wheeling his arms through the air, he pranced down the street, still laughing. He reminded Rush of the sophomores who'd laughed at him on his first day in high school: "So you don't know what you're getting into, huh? Boy, are you in for surprises!"

What kind of barbershop is this? Rush thought. He looked into the light coming out of the open door and stepped warily inside.

He descended a rickety spiral stairway down a long, musty stone shaft. The air was thick and damp as a cave, with the cool antiseptic aroma of a doctor's office.

At the bottom of the shaft, Rush saw a vast bright chamber. Except for the concrete walls, it looked like the living room of an eccentric curio collector. Thick books lay on heavy tables, and a gold and black Oriental rug ran along the hardwood floor down the length of the room. On tables with octopuslike legs, lamps of snaky, curving shapes illuminated objects displayed on the walls; a tiny skull with three eye sockets, a recipe for Dangerous Soup, a pair of red-stained vampire fangs.

Near Rush stood shining steel cases of brightly colored hair tonics. At least Rush assumed that they were hair tonics, although he'd never seen tonics that glowed green, or looked thick as honey, or resembled any of the several dozen other fluids that filled the glass bottles.

In the center of the room stood an old-fashioned barber chair, its back to Rush, with black leather cushions nailed to a mahogany frame. A man sat silently in the chair. Rush could see nothing of him except the pink top of his balding scalp, surrounded by a corona of unkempt gray hair.

Rush tried not to stammer. "Excuse me," he said, "I'm looking for the guy who—"

"You've found him," said the man in a rich melodic baritone. If a gong could speak, it would sound like that man's resonant voice. The man slowly spun around in the chair. He looked to Rush like a happy, clever gnome. He was short and stocky, with an enormous head. His scraggly hair wiggled down to his shoulders, and his curly

74

beard hid half of his face. His crescent-shaped eyebrows bounced up and down every time he spoke. He seemed old, but full of energy, with bouncy movements and eyes that danced.

The man wore a heavy long-sleeved white tunic that combined elements of a barber's smock, a surgeon's coveralls and a lunatic's straitjacket. He held a small black book with no title. In fact, there was no printing on the cover at all. Over his wrist lay a white towel, the kind that a barber would douse in hot water and lay on the face of a customer waiting to be shaved.

"Vink's the name," the man continued. Emphasizing every syllable, he added, "Dr. Vink."

"Dr. Vink?" Rush asked. His heart sank. *This old hairbag's going to save Max from that giant ghost?*

Dr. Vink seemed delighted. "Precisely!" he exclaimed, as if Rush were the first person who had ever pronounced his name right. He clapped the book shut.

What's with this guy? Rush thought. He recalled the laughing man with the gray suit and frizzy hair. *I guess he's not used to people who can think straight.*

Dr. Vink ambled over to Rush with a springy, rhythmic gait, almost dancing. As he approached,

75

Rush noticed stains of rainbow fluid splattered on his overalls. The man wrapped a hand around Rush's shoulder and gently propelled him toward the barber chair.

In a low rumble, Dr. Vink announced, "I've been waiting for you."

76

CHAPTER 9

"You have?" Rush asked. He wanted to pull back, but the barber's grip was surprisingly strong.

"What do you think of my latest endeavor?" Dr. Vink asked, waving the book around the room in a sweeping arc.

Rush didn't know what to answer. What latest endeavor? Did he mean the barber shop? Maybe cutting hair was only the most recent of who knows how many weird jobs. Dr. Vink didn't seem stable enough to keep any career for very long.

Besides, who cared? The giant ghost could be slicing Max open right now!

Rush tried to speak up, but the barber spoke

first. "Of course," he said, "patrons are less interested in coiffure . . ." He whacked the smooth
seat of the barber chair with his cloth; Rush sat
down, holding the spyglass in his lap. "Than they
are in my unique hair tonics." Dr. Vink turned
the barber chair toward a mirror embedded in
the wall. He laid his book and towel on a steel
counter nearby.

On the counter stood a bottle filled with a bubbling blue liquid. Dr. Vink picked up the bottle
and pulled off the stopper; an aroma like human
skin floated out. Dr. Vink continued breathlessly,
"They have such interesting properties." He in-
haled the odor deeply and shivered with delight.
With wild enthusiasm, he asked, "Shall I massage
a few drops into your scalp?"

"Uhhh . . ." Rush pushed himself back into the
chair, away from the man's insane grin. *Don't
touch me, you old whacko!* "No, thanks."

At that, Dr. Vink sobered up. "Of course not,"
he agreed firmly. He replaced the stopper. "We
have work to do." He bounced across the room
and turned away from Rush to deposit the bottle
in one of the steel cabinets near the doorway.

I don't have time for this! Rush thought. He
spun the chair around and faced Dr. Vink.
"Look," Rush said, "my little brother's in trouble,
and—"

"I know all about your brother," Dr. Vink said with calm authority, pulling himself up to his full height. He folded his hands over his chest and allowed himself a tight-lipped smile. "And I can help you find him. As long as you understand one thing."

"What's that?"

Dr. Vink whirled and glared at Rush with wild eyes. In an indignant tone, he declared, "I am not a nutbag!"

He scurried past the barber chair. Confused, Rush turned to watch him. "How do you know about—"

"Jonas Cutter," Dr. Vink announced. Standing by an old desk covered with stacks of ancient books and brittle yellowing parchments, he reminded Rush of a history teacher announcing the subject of that day's lecture.

The doctor snapped his fingers and looked up from his documents, as if saying Cutter's name reminded him of a long-dormant memory. "Captain Jonas Cutter, he called himself." He picked up the top book of a teetering pile and flipped through the pages, searching. "A murderous galley slave who led the bloodiest mutiny in maritime history."

Dr. Vink shut the book and put it back down. Apparently, it hadn't given him the information

79

that he needed. He picked up a shaving razor that lay atop another tower of books. "He and his murderous band fed a crew of sailors to the sharks, captured their ship, and then went on to a vile career of piracy and thievery."

The barber grabbed a piece of paper—Rush noticed that it was a Magic Mansion flyer—from a batch of documents. He turned to Rush. "They say he took the name Cutter because of his love for the blade . . ." Dr. Vink raised the razor; it flashed in the light. "And what it could do to flesh." With one stroke, Dr. Vink sliced the paper neatly down the center.

Rush stared. *What's all this supposed to mean?*

Dr. Vink turned back to the table and laid the razor and paper down. As he talked, he took one book after another off of a particularly tall stack. "History says he concealed an immense treasure in a secret vault that to this day has never been found." He picked up a large musty volume near the bottom of the pile.

Rush scowled. The old troll was going on about buried treasure when Max was in danger. "Why are you telling me this?"

"Because I do believe," Dr. Vink answered, "I've tracked the beggar down." He wheeled, opened the book, and thrust it at Rush. On one page was an ink sketch of a giant bearish man in a long coat, raising a sword. The man's head was enormous, with glaring eyes. Scarred skin partly covered the right eye.

Rush bolted toward the book. "That's the guy!" He looked up at Dr. Vink. "We gotta tell the cops." He spun and took off for the doorway.

"The police can't help you, lad," Dr. Vink said.

Rush stopped and turned. The doctor seemed confident. Rush's hot eagerness drained away. He turned back slowly. "Why not?"

"Because," Dr. Vink replied, "Jonas Cutter has been dead for two hundred years."

Rush's face turned pale. He closed his eyes and slumped wearily back into the barber chair. "I don't believe this."

"Don't be discouraged," Dr. Vink chirped.

Yeah, sure, Rush thought. *You try not being discouraged. It's not your brother who's been kidnapped by ghosts.* He opened his eyes.

Dr. Vink set his book down carefully and bustled over to Rush. In a low husky tone, as if confiding a deep secret, the barber went on, "This is all according to plan."

Rush looked up. *Enough guessing games!* "What plan? Whose plan?"

Dr. Vink laid a hand on Rush's shoulder. It was apparently meant to be comforting, but any contact from the strange little man made Rush

81

uneasy. The doctor paced on tiptoe around the barber chair, unable to contain his joy. "After decades of searching every nautical rat hole from the Caribbean to Prince Edward Island"—his voice dropped to an awed whisper and he stared into the distance with wonderment—"I believe I've discovered the lost treasure of Captain Cutter." Through the corners of his eyes, Dr. Vink shot Rush a sneaky glance and pointed at the spyglass in Rush's lap. "And it's right here. In this very town!"

Rush looked up, only half believing the man. "Where?"

Dr. Vink seemed surprised that Rush had to ask. "I don't know." He picked up the spyglass and patted it. "But you do." He took the spyglass to his table of books.

"What?" Rush asked. *Sardo's right,* he thought. *This guy really is a nutbag.*

Dr. Vink laid the little tube between two stacks of books. "This spyglass is the key," he responded, perfectly calm again. "It is a window into a supernatural world that only you can see."

"But why me? I don't get—"

"Cutter vowed to protect his treasure for all eternity." Dr. Vink bent down. He reached under the table and brought up a treasure chest that Rush recognized immediately with a burst of shock. Before Rush could speak, the doctor went on. "They say his ghost stands guard to this day." He placed the box on a short pile of books and touched the lid. "This chest belonged to the one man who tried to defeat Cutter—but instead met with a grisly death."

Rush couldn't hold himself back any longer. "That's from the Magic Mansion!"

"I left it there myself, hoping to find the Champion."

"Who?" Rush asked. *Oh, great. Just when the old vaporhead's starting to make sense, he goes off into outer space again. What does this have to do with Max?*

Dr. Vink opened the chest's lid. "Before he died, this brave soul vowed that one day a champion would come to avenge the deaths of all of Cutter's victims."

Rush licked his suddenly dry lips and found himself breathing more heavily. With sudden dread, he saw where Dr. Vink was heading. The barber reached into the chest and pulled out a dagger—the grimy, rusty blade that Rush had found when he'd first opened the chest.

"These tools were empowered by the souls of those victims," Dr. Vink said, placing the dagger back in the chest. "Legend says that whoever opened the chest to retrieve them would be the one"—he closed the chest—"to do battle."

Rush had been alarmed when Max was kidnapped, worried when he ran to the Magic Mansion, apprehensive on Prospect Street, confused and even shocked in the presence of Dr. Vink. But he hadn't felt true, shuddering panic until now.

Go back and fight that Goliath with the scarred eye and the ferocious grin? The mountainous terror with a shout like thunder, the one who laughed as if Rush were a baby challenging an army? The wild grizzly who killed hardened sailors?

Rush stared at Dr. Vink and couldn't move. He felt freezing cold. "No." He shook his head. "No way."

Dr. Vink picked up the chest and walked toward Rush. "You opened the chest, didn't you?" he challenged.

Rush wanted to run. "Yeah, but—"

"What's your name?" Dr. Vink demanded with a fierce glare. "Your full name."

At last, a question Rush could handle. "Russell Ian Keegan." He stared back defiantly at Dr. Vink. "So what?"

Dr. Vink flipped over the chest. Carved crudely into the bottom were the words IAN KEEGAN. Rush gulped.

"This belonged to your ancestor," the doctor

84

insisted. He leaned down toward Rush, his voice shaking with excitement. "You are the one, lad." With wild fervor, the man shouted, "You have to finish what he began two hundred years ago!"

"Forget it!" Rush said. "I'm just a kid!"

Dr. Vink stared as if he couldn't accept Rush's words. He straightened up and tossed his head back, his face haughty and cold, as if he were an aristocrat about to order a rude guest out of the manor. "Perhaps you're right." He clipped the words off with immense dignity.

The old occultist turned his back on Rush and strolled to the book-covered table. He gazed into space with a thoughtful expression and went on in a quiet, conversational tone. "I suppose it's easier to hide behind the veil of youth"—he placed the chest on the table and stared thoughtfully into space—"than to face the responsibility of a brother you despise."

The words stung like a slap. Rush shot out of the chair, furious. "I don't despise Max! I want him back!"

Dr. Vink turned to Rush with the confident glee of a card shark with four aces. "Then accept your destiny," he answered, firm and strong.

The two silently watched each other. *I want Max back,* Rush thought, *but this way?*

He could feel his heart beating like a jackhammer. His palms were slick with sweat.

85

Dr. Vink slowly turned back to the chest and raised its lid. Rush watched in dread, as if a snake were coiled inside, rearing back, waiting for the moment to strike. With his heart racing, he stepped forward until he was close enough to touch the old box.

Rush hesitated—*What do I do now?*—and looked up at Dr. Vink. The old man nodded toward the dark cobwebbed chest.

Rush reached in and picked up the dagger. It was as grimy and decrepit as ever.

It began to glow. The blade changed from gray to a gleaming, mirrored silver. Red and blue jewels emerged from inside the blade like submerged eggs floating to the surface of a gleaming lake.

The black handle wavered and shimmered; when it grew solid again, the black surface shone. It fit Rush's hand as if it had been carved for him alone.

To get a better look, Rush raised the dagger to the light; the blade glimmered and flashed. Dr. Vink smiled proudly. "Now," he said, "tell me what you saw through the spyglass."

Elsewhere, someone was holding a larger, sharper blade. Jonas Cutter was sharpening his favorite and deadliest saber: the one that had killed Ian Keegan.

His foot rapidly pumped the ancient pedal that turned the granite whetting wheel. Sparks flew and a rough squeal filled the room as he slid the blade along the whirling gray surface with a sure, steady rhythm, back and forth, honing the steel edge.

Behind him hung a huge birdcage, eight feet tall. Black cables as thick as fists held the cage to the ceiling.

Cutter had had the cage built to humiliate prisoners. Cooping a man up and displaying him before the crew like a pet parakeet was cruel enough to weaken even the roughest mutineer. And Cutter found it great sport to hoist the cage to the highest mast, let it drop, watch it sink into the ocean—and raise it again only when the man inside had drowned, pounding in desperation against the wrought-iron bars as his lungs filled with water.

Sitting inside the cage, Max gripped the dark cold bars. Now that the boy was firmly imprisoned, Cutter had no more need to keep him hypnotized. He wanted Max to feel the danger that surrounded him.

With worried eyes, Max watched Cutter's powerful hand hold the saber. He could smell the hot bitter air rising from the friction of whetstone and blade.

Cutter spoke over the noisy whine of grinding

steel on stone. A thin crafty smile replaced the wild gleeful passion that he'd displayed earlier. "The end is near, young one." He let out a low chuckle.

Max shivered in the heat, staring at the blade as it grew sharper and sharper.

INGREDIENTS: May contain FD&C Yellow #5, FD&C Yellow #6, FD&C Blue #1, FD&C Red #28 and Hydroxpropyl Methylcellulose, All ink colorants are FDA certified and non-toxic

Manufactured by Meyer Label Co., Inc., Englewood NJ.

DIRECTIONS FOR APPLYING TATTOOS

1. Cut out tattoo you wish to apply
2. Lightly wet skin (for best results use soapy water)
3. Place tattoo face down on wet area
4. Apply pressure for approximately 5 seconds and lift pap
5. Remove with soap, water & wash cloth

CHAPTER

10

An hour later, Rush gazed through the spyglass, examining the cemetery that he'd seen in his nightmare. Searching for clues, he shifted the tube right and left.

He lowered the spyglass. The gray tombstones and moonlit grass stretched out before him.

"A cemetery!" exulted Dr. Vink. "Perfect!" Standing at Rush's side, he gazed down at the dark fields before them.

Dr. Vink had found the cemetery more easily than Rush had expected. Back in the barbershop, Rush described the view that he'd seen through the spyglass. Dr. Vink dove into his pile of books like a dog digging up a bone, tossing tomes and papers behind him, while Rush hoped that the doctor knew what he was doing.

Dr. Vink pulled out a particularly heavy book and blew off years of dust. A skeleton, embossed in silver, lay on the book's black cover. Below the bones, Rush read the words *Prominent Tombs and Mausoleums, Volume IX.*

With shaky, excited hands, Dr. Vink snapped the book open and pressed a stubby finger down on a page near the end.

"Is this the place that you saw?" he asked with a sly, knowing smile.

Rush looked over Dr. Vink's shoulder and saw a pencil rendering of the mausoleum where Cutter had taken Max. Stunned, he couldn't speak but only nodded.

"Ah-ha!" Dr. Vink shouted. "Off we go, lad. Off to rescue your brother." His voice suddenly turned dark. "And defeat the blackguard Cutter."

With Rush alongside him, Dr. Vink drove his rattletrap '64 Tepes roadster out of town at top speed. He turned off the main road onto a concrete driveway, passing under a sign that read PROSPECT MEMORIAL FUNERAL HOME. The driveway ended at the foot of a grassy rise. Dr. Vink braked hard, nearly sending Rush through the windshield.

While Dr. Vink pulled Ian Keegan's chest from

the car's trunk, Rush got out of the car. He picked up the spyglass and walked up the rise; from there, he could see the entire cemetery. He peered through the spyglass.

It was at that point that Dr. Vink joined him. He laid Cutter's chest on the ground.

"Perfect!" he repeated. "This is the oldest cemetery in the state, lad. Cutter could bury box after box of treasure here, and no one would suspect a thing. After all, people bury boxes here all the time." A grin split the doctor's broad face. "Oh, that Cutter was a clever one."

Rush didn't want to hear any praise for the pirate's prowess. "Now what do we do?"

Dr. Vink turned calmer, more professorial. "The spyglass"—he plucked it from Rush's hand—"brought you here. You'll need these to continue." He reached into the chest and handed Rush the old blackened key. He reached down again and brought up the gleaming dagger.

"What do I do with them?" Rush asked, perplexed.

"You'll know"—he raised the dagger to Rush's face and slapped it into his hand—"when the time comes."

More mysteries, Rush thought as he slid the key into his back pocket. *What is it with this guy?* "Why are you doing all this?"

91

Dr. Vink sucked in a deep breath. His eyes took on a faraway look. "If all goes well, a few pieces of treasure will help to fund some of my . . ." He chuckled. "Unique endeavors."

Rush slipped the dagger between his belt and pants. *Great. Max and I could die so he can do some nutbar research.* "And if all doesn't go well?"

Dr. Vink looked back at Rush. In a fierce, husky tone, he commanded, "It must!" He leaned in close. "It's your destiny."

Rush pulled the dagger from his belt and looked at it. *Am I really supposed to beat a ghost with this little thing?* He turned to face Dr. Vink. "But what if—"

Dr. Vink was gone.

Rush turned around, scanning the entire field of tombstones. "Hey!" No place nearby was large enough to hide a grown man. "Dr. Vink?"

The old mystic had vanished like a popped soap bubble. *Don't pull tricks now!* Rush thought. *I need help!*

But the doctor was gone. Rush slipped the dagger back into his belt and walked down a short flight of stone steps toward the graves.

He passed a tall hedge and a stone pedestal. A strange feeling crept over him. "I've done this before," he said to himself. "It's like my dream. That means . . ."

92

He stopped to remember. *It means my next stop's the mausoleum. If everything's just like my dream, it ought to be straight ahead.* He looked around to find the building.

"Grandson!" said a voice behind him.

Rush spun. The ghost from his nightmare was staring at him.

The ghost looked worse than he had in Rush's dream. His face was grimy and his head tilted to one side, as if the bloody slash in his neck had cut the muscles that allowed him to lift it.

You're not supposed to be here, Rush thought. *You're supposed to show up at the mausoleum! What's going on here?*

Rush managed to speak. "Who are you?"

The man floated toward him. "Sure, you know who I am," he said with a light Irish accent. His voice echoed in the still night.

Rush took a guess. "Ian Keegan?" *What'll he do if I'm wrong?*

The ghost nodded. He seemed weak; his head bent down and he had a hard time lifting it. He pointed a weak hand forward and floated past Rush, wafting deeper into the cemetery. Rush mustered his courage and followed him.

The two Keegans did not see the white fog roll quietly behind them with Mr. Noise inside, watching.

The ghost reeled; he seemed on the verge of fainting. His mouth opened and closed several times as he tried to speak. Rush wanted to help him but couldn't imagine how.

At last, the ghost spoke, "I placed a curse upon Jonas Cutter." He pointed forward. Before them stood the mausoleum, shaded by overhanging trees. "You must fulfill that curse."

"Oh, man." Rush groaned. "Look, I don't know about any curse." The ghost looked at him blankly; he didn't seem to have expected Rush to talk back. Rush explained, "All I want is my brother back."

The ghost took in the words. Then he said softly, "The dagger has the power."

What's that supposed to mean? Rush looked down at the dagger and fingered its handle. It seemed so small, not powerful at all. He looked up at his ancestor.

Before Rush could ask another question, the ghost pointed at the mausoleum.

He's right, Rush thought. *I gotta get in there and save Max. There's no time for questions.* He took a deep breath and headed slowly toward the building's massive door. *Cutter, here I come.*

"Grandson?"

Rush whirled. *You do wanna talk! Tell me something I can use!* The ghost looked terribly

94

tired. His head leaned to one side, as if he couldn't muster the strength to hold it upright. "Do not be fooled. What he wants is not what he desires."

Rush sighed. He'd been through this before, during his nightmare, and didn't like it then. "What does that mean?"

"All our hopes go wi' ya." The ghost waved.

"Don't go!" Rush pleaded. "You gotta help me!"

The ghost was gone.

Rush started walking to the mausoleum, looking up in every direction, alert for anything strange. He expected vines to shoot up his legs and Cutter to stamp through the doorway.

Nothing happened. He approached the mausoleum's enormous door and pulled the key from his back pocket. *Here I go, right into Cutter's hands.*

He slipped the key into the door's tall black lock. It turned slowly, with dull metallic clunks that echoed in the room beyond.

The door handle, a long bronze curve, had been built for Cutter's massive hand. Rush grabbed it with both fists and pulled.

The door resisted, two hundred years of cobwebs and mildew holding it closed. Rush yanked again; it pulled forward a few inches, creaking.

With knees knocking, Rush stepped inside. The door shut behind him, sealing him in.

The room was dark. Its shadowy stone walls met at sharp angles and tight corners. Thin lines of white moonlight flowed through gaps between the roof slats and ran along the dim gray bricks. Jagged columns jutted out from the walls, thrusting rocky edges toward Rush. Coffins lay in nooks carved into the wall, their once shiny veneer as gray and dull as the stone room around them. Vines and thin branches snaked through the roof and floor, their woody fingers reaching through the darkness.

Rush looked around the room and pushed branches aside. Max wasn't there. Neither were Cutter or Mr. Noise.

"Grandson?" came a familiar voice.

You're back! Rush thought. He looked around for Ian Keegan, but the ghost wasn't there.

"Look everywhere." Keegan's voice echoed in the chamber. It faded into silence.

But what am I looking for? Rush wondered. "You've gotta help me!"

There was no answer. *Okay, fine. You want me to look everywhere? I'll look right here.* He reached toward one of the coffins. The cobweb-covered lid groaned as Rush lifted it.

Rush expected Cutter to leap out. Instead, he found a pile of human bones. A lifeless skull lay on its side like an empty vase knocked over by a careless child. A rib cage, soiled by thin layers of grime and covered by the tattered scraps of a black burial suit, had apparently gone undisturbed for decades.

"Yuck." Rush grunted. *"Look everywhere,"* *huh? Thanks, Ian.*

And then Rush saw something that sent him reeling backward, gasping.

The skull was turning to face him.

CHAPTER
11

"Welcome aboard, skipper," the skull said in the gleeful voice of Captain Jonas Cutter. It laughed, filling the room with fat whirling screeches.

Rush's eyes bulged and his heart hammered. He backed away, not seeing the long black crack in the middle of the room.

The floor fell out from under Rush's feet. The skeleton continued to laugh, filling the room with a storm of cackles, while Rush fell screaming into the blackness. The air whistled in his ears as he plummeted, his arms and legs flailing.

He hit something rough but yielding. It collapsed under his weight, and he slammed hard into a rock floor.

Rush flung his arms over his face to protect himself from attack. The move hurt; banging into the floor had bruised his shoulders. As he lay waiting for the pain to subside, Rush listened hard, but he heard nothing. He lowered his arms and looked around.

A long wooden pole lay over his leg. He shoved it off and scrambled to his feet, ready for Cutter to attack.

He looked around. *Where am I?*

He saw a round chamber, wide as the Keegan front lawn. It was an enormous cavern with walls and floor of solid rock. The walls, covered with old dry branches and vines, were pock-marked with shadowy crannies—some fist-size, others as tall as doorways and deep enough to enter.

In the stone ceiling was a square hole, hinged at either side. Two oak panels hung down from the hinges. *A trapdoor,* Rush realized. *I fell through a trapdoor!*

At his feet lay the pole that he'd shoved off, plus three others. They were polished tree trunks, at least ten feet long, tied to the corners of a fishing net. They'd propped up the net and held it taut until Rush had fallen into it, knocking the flimsy structure down.

Rush looked over his shoulder. Thick vines dangled from the floor of the mausoleum, through the trapdoor, and down the chamber's rocky wall to the floor. Near some of the vines stood a makeshift ladder.

Rush approached the ladder. It leaned against the wall and led up to the trapdoor. *Can I use this thing to get Max out?*

It didn't look likely. The ladder's rungs were old sticks, its poles a pair of long thin tree trunks. The ropes that tied the rungs to the poles looked weak from age. Only one frayed, brittle cord, which tied the ladder to the wall, kept the structure from falling. It looked as though the rickety, brittle thing might collapse under his weight.

Rush sighed. "Swell," he muttered.

"Not leaving so soon, are ya?"

Cutter! Rush jumped away from the ladder and looked around for the pirate. The big man was nowhere in sight.

In low, teasing tones, Cutter said, "You just came aboard." His voice echoed through the cavern, surrounding his victim.

Rush kept walking, looking up at every angle. The voice seemed to come from everywhere. He felt like a fawn in a hunter's gunsight. "I . . . I know who you are," he said, trying to sound brave.

100

"Do ya now?" Cutter asked. He laughed, amused that his victim thought himself so clever. "Then let's see if you can find me."

Rush circled the room. Alert for ambushes, he kept his back to the walls.

Behind him lay one of the deeper nooks: the mouth of a rocky tunnel. Around a bend deep inside, a light flickered.

That's it! Rush ran toward the light.

Steel points shot toward his face. A heavy gate dropped from the roof of the tunnel, its sharp tips nearly slicing his skin.

With a dull, echoing clang, the gate hit the ground and cut Rush off from the light. Rush's jaw dropped. *Cutter,* he thought. *He controls everything here!*

Rush backpedaled into the middle of the chamber. He swung around right and left, searching for a new exit.

"Pity," said Cutter with a pitiless voice. Rush could imagine his cruel, smug grin. "Yer first choice was a poor one," Cutter added. "Not a good start."

Rush listened for more but heard nothing. He turned slowly, hunting for a new way out.

Something in the wall behind him began to glow. Rush turned to see the mouth of another tunnel; a yellow light burned around a bend deep within. Slowly, watching for falling gates, Rush stepped inside.

The tunnel was damp. Branches, vines, and dewy moss dripping sap and water covered its rounded, bulbous walls. Soggy leaves carpeted the floor. Although a fine mist cooled the air, Rush was sweating.

He looked ahead. From around a curve, the light was still shining. He followed it.

"Oh, careful, now," came Cutter's teasing voice.

Careful about what? Rush turned to find out, and the sight sent him stumbling into a wall, gasping.

A skeleton hung on the other side of the tunnel, a spear jammed through its neck.

"Got the point?" Cutter laughed, sending rolls of nasty glee echoing through the tunnel.

The skeleton's head nearly touched the cave's high ceiling, and its feet barely grazed the floor. Whoever had lived in that skeleton, he'd been big, and undoubtedly strong; to get this far meant that he must have been brave.

And Cutter had killed him as soon as he'd walked in.

Rush shivered. He didn't feel big, strong, or

brave. He clenched his sweaty hands to keep them from trembling. "Look, I'm no hero! I don't wanna hurt you or anything."

Cutter laughed with delight. "Oh, does I sound afraid?"

Heck, no, Rush thought. His heart drummed; his gut felt knotted and twisted. He checked back over his shoulder, expecting an attack like the one that had killed the skeleton. No one was there— at least no one he could see.

Rush stepped forward slowly. He wondered what the next danger would be. Another trapdoor? A gate to slice him in two? Cutter himself?

He did not notice the thing at his feet that was set to kill him.

As he gazed around the cave, Rush stepped forward and felt something tug at his leg. He looked down to see his foot pushing a thin vine stretched between the cave walls. He heard something snap in the cave wall by his right ear and turned toward the sound.

He saw a steel spear aimed at his eyes.

The spear flew at Rush as he dove forward, rolling into a somersault on the cold ground. He sat for a moment, panting. *What was that?* Behind him, something rumbled loudly.

Several spikes—at the perfect height to skewer

103

his eyes, heart, and stomach—had crashed into the left side of the tunnel. They slowly receded into dark holes in the right wall, making a scratching noise as they went.

From the top spike dangled a decayed human head: the deathtrap's latest victim. As the spike slid back into its slot, the head swung on its sharp tip, as if to tell Rush, "No, you don't want to keep going. Look what happened to me."

That could've been me, Rush thought. He turned away; he couldn't stand to look at the thing.

"Mmm, this is gettin' interesting," Cutter's voice teased. Rush tried to ignore him. He stood and kept walking down the dank cave, but he couldn't stop Cutter from chuckling at him. "Let's see what other fires we can start."

Someone laughed, but it wasn't Cutter. Rush froze.

In a deep offshoot of the tunnel, a giant gray cannon was pointed directly at Rush. Next to it stood a ragged, ghostly sailor, snickering loudly. He touched a torch to the cannon's black coiled fuse.

A cannonball shot out. As Rush ducked behind a large rock, the projectile whizzed past his head, trailing smoke as it flew. Rush lay flat on the ground and waited for more.

The tunnel fell silent. Rush raised his head to peer through the bitter smoke. He looked at the jagged hole that the cannonball had made—exactly the size of his own head—and gulped.

But the cannonball itself was gone. So was the cannon. So was the sailor.

Who the heck was that? Rush wondered. *Had to be one of Cutter's goons. Well, at least he's not here anymore.*

Or was he? Rush heard someone walking toward him from the cavern ahead. He leaned forward, straining desperately to see the person's face through the thick smoke.

"Max!" Rush shouted.

Rush scrambled to his feet. Coughing through the slowly clearing smoke, he ran to his brother. "Max, are you okay?"

Max nodded weakly. He didn't look okay. His eyes were half closed, as if from fatigue; he trudged toward Rush slowly, dragging his feet. His posture was slack and his shoulders limp and slumped.

I don't know what Cutter did to you, Rush thought, *but he's not gonna do it again.* "C'mon," Rush commanded. "Let's go." He grabbed Max's wrist and started running back toward the big chamber and its still-open trapdoor. He started

105

planning a way out: *If the ladder's too shaky, maybe we can climb the walls.*

Max jerked him back. Rush swiveled to shout, "Come on, what's the—"

Rush looked straight into the leering face of Mr. Noise.

CHAPTER 12

With a flick of his wrist, the pirate shoved Rush to the leaf-covered ground. He lay helpless on his back, like an upended turtle.

Rush trembled at the man's demonic grin.

Leaning down toward Rush's terrified face, Mr. Noise let out a sinister, raspy wheeze and crowed, "Nice to see you again, laddie!" The sailor reached for a long sword hanging at his waist.

"Sorry." Mr. Noise growled as he pulled the sword from its scabbard. He glanced at its blood-stained blade and turned his murderous gaze back down to Rush. "Just doin' me job." He raised the sword high over his victim.

Rush looked around, searching desperately for

anything to stop Mr. Noise. He saw the tunnel's walls and the leaves on its floor—and amid the leaves, a miracle.

It was the dagger. It must have jogged loose when he hit the ground. He grasped the handle in a shivering wet palm.

Mr. Noise laughed again. The dagger's blade was not much longer than Rush's hand, while Mr. Noise's saber was the size of a baseball bat—and the sailor wielded it with an expert's supple strength. As the villian's sword was poised for a killing thrust, Rush, shuddering, lifted the dagger.

The tiny blade began to glow and vibrate. A blinding ball of light exploded from the tip.

It flew into Mr. Noise's face. The sailor flailed as if a prizefighter were pummeling him and twitched as if he'd grabbed a live wire. The glow spread all over his body.

With an agonized yelp, he disappeared.

Rush stared at the dust floating in the cool air where Mr. Noise had stood, gaping at the still-glowing dagger as it faded back to normal. *The dagger killed him. But he's a ghost!*

He remembered Ian Keegan's words: "The dagger has the power."

He scrambled to his feet and slipped the dagger back into his belt. Peering into the gloom, he carefully rounded another bend in the tunnel. It

108

was cold there, and cramped, with a lower ceiling and tighter walls. He looked over his shoulder, alert for another ambush.

A light shone up ahead. Rush crept closer.

The light came from an arched opening in the stone wall. In the arch stood a thick door of heavy oak—the same door that Ian Keegan had entered, carrying the dagger, two hundred years before. Rush pushed the door open and entered the room where his ancestor had been killed.

The room was enormous. Even larger than the chamber beneath the trapdoor, the room was as big as a house, with alcoves and hollows as deep as walk-in closets.

And it held more riches than Rush had ever seen in his life. Lush tapestries and pearl necklaces lay strewn over desk-size crates filled with mahogany sculptures. On a bed of gold doubloons stood silver goblets and jewel-speckled crowns. Tall plush chairs from an emperor's dining hall stood around the room. Rubies and emeralds overflowed from nautical barrels stolen from Portuguese freighters and Spanish galleons. Candles flickered in elaborate, hand-fashioned candelabra, sending a golden glow over paintings of princesses and kings. An oversize birdcage hung from thick cables. Inside, a prisoner with half-closed eyes sat against the bars.

Suddenly, the prisoner clambered to his feet. "Rush!" he called in a familiar voice.

Max!

The younger boy grabbed the bars to balance himself as the cage swayed under him.

Rush strode toward his brother, then stopped, just out of arm's reach. "It's really you, isn't it?" he asked suspiciously.

"Yeah, get me outta here!" Max cried in that familiar high-pitched wail he always slid into when Rush doubted him. He'd heard it back home when Max had insisted that there was a skeleton under the bed. There was no doubt: this was not Mr. Noise in disguise, but Max himself.

The door to Max's cage had no lock, but Cutter had looped heavy ropes around the bars and tied them in sailor's knots to hold the door closed. Rush turned and pulled the scratchy cords, trying to undo the tight tangles.

"I didn't think you were gonna come," Max said softly, gazing at him with sad eyes.

Rush grimaced and turned away. Max's comment insulted him, confused him, and made him feel guilty, all at the same time. He concentrated on the ropes and tried to sound rough and uncaring as he asked, "What are you talking about?"

"You said you hated me."

The comment hung in the air. Rush dropped the ropes. He knew that Max was right.

110

Max watched him, waiting for an explanation.

"Look, Max," Rush began uneasily, "I said a lot of stupid things I didn't mean. I'm sorry."

Max looked down, taking it all in, unsure of how to accept the words.

Rush stared at his baby brother, kidnapped and captive in a cage. After all that had happened, "sorry" wasn't good enough. *I shouldn't've blown him off back home when he said that stupid spyglass was moving by itself. Heck, I shouldn't've cut him off after we ditched Mrs. Gregory.*

Ditching Mrs. Gregory . . . Rush smiled. He bent down and tried to catch Max's eye. "Can I be on your team again?"

Max slowly looked up, a smile spreading across his features like a sunrise. Rush relaxed for the first time in hours.

Behind his back, a familiar voice chuckled.

Rush whirled. In a tall plush chair on a nearby rock ledge, Cutter was slashing a carving knife into an oak branch; chips of wood fell with each chop.

Rush blinked. *It's not possible.* He had seen the chair when he came in. Cutter hadn't been there.

But he was there now.

"Touchin'. Very touchin'." Cutter snarled through gritted teeth, trying to restrain a frenzied anger. He hacked at the branch again, and sharp-

111

edged hunks flew like sparks. Rush could imagine that knife chopping into his own neck or into Max's. He backed away and grabbed a bar of the cage to steady himself.

Cutter pounded the knife harder and faster, his massive body shaking. "I am so moved, I could almost *die!*" he shrieked. He stopped slamming the knife and glared at Rush with fury.

Rush swallowed. His throat was dry as sand as he opened his mouth to make a speech that would ease Cutter's rage and make him let them go.

He couldn't think of anything to say.

"But then again," Cutter went on, "I am already dead." He swung his arm to indicate a dark corner of the cave.

A huge skeleton lay in the corner, dressed in Cutter's naval outfit. While the man wielding the knife wore a jacket of rich deep blue, as fresh as the day it was dyed, the skeleton's coat had faded to a dusty black. The skeleton wore a captain's hat; its pants had decayed to scraps and lay on the ground around its leg bones. On the skeleton's hand was a ring bearing a giant blue sapphire. An identical ring flashed on the hand wielding the big knife.

Suddenly sick, Rush couldn't stand to look at the skeleton. He turned back to Cutter—*no,* he

112

told himself, *Cutter's ghost*. "Look," he pleaded, "I don't want any trouble."

Cutter stood, staring in disbelief. "You went through all the trouble of tracking me down!" He rose from his chair and headed toward the rim of the ledge. "You went through the trouble of running my gauntlet and dispatchin' Mr. Noise!" His voice rose to a wild roar, and he pounded his chest. "You went through all the trouble of breaking into *my treasure room*!"

Rush tried to speak, but Cutter kept yelling, his features twisting with rage. "Yes, I think you're looking for trouble, and skipper"—the big man leaped off the ledge—"you've found it!"

Rush swallowed again and nearly gagged. "Look," he protested, "I didn't want any part of this." Rush sidled away, passing in front of a candelabrum and a sailing ship's deck stool.

Cutter followed him closely, keeping pace with every step, watching every move with the focused gaze of a cobra preparing to strike. The big man raised his arms, ready to grab his prey. Rush tried to keep calm. "You're the one who—"

"I've stood guard here for two centuries," Cutter said, snarling, "waitin' for ya to come!" He added with bloodthirsty glee, "Waitin' for the grand battle!" He spread his arms wide as if inviting Rush to attack.

113

"I don't want to fight!" Rush shouted. *Doesn't this monster get it?*

Cutter grinned. "Then you've come to the wrong place." He nodded, as if agreeing with himself, and laughed. He turned and stepped up to another ledge.

On the ledge stood a wooden table covered in souvenirs of Cutter's seafaring life: scrolled parchment maps, a ship's wheel, a barrel of doubloons—and a long scabbard with a sword handle sticking out. As Rush watched, uncertain of what to do, Cutter stopped laughing.

"The fight will be a fair one," Cutter explained calmly, as if to himself. The words sounded formal, rehearsed. He had apparently planned the fight a thousand times.

As the brothers and the pirate concentrated on the battle to come, they did not notice Dr. Vink slip silently through the cavern's door.

Cutter laid his enormous hand on the sword handle. The pirate drew his saber out slowly, relishing each gleaming inch, savoring the slow scrape as the blade slid from the scabbard's hardwood interior. "I think swords will do just fine." He ran his thumb along the sharp steel edge and studied the blade as it flashed in the candlelight.

With nothing at hand but a candelabrum and deck stool, Rush stammered, "I . . . I don't have a sword." *Please, God, let that stop him. He wants a grand battle; I can't give him one!*

Cutter said nothing. He grinned and chuckled to himself, nodding. Finally, still grinning, he said one word: "Pity."

He whirled to face Rush. "Then you really are in trouble!" With a laugh, he leaped off the ledge and whipped his sword at Rush's neck.

CHAPTER 13

Rush backpedaled from the swinging sword and tripped over the deck stool. Cutter hurled himself forward, thrusting the saber again and again toward Rush's unprotected eyes.

Rush hefted the stool into the saber's path. The blade hit, and Rush felt vibrations from the impact shoot up his arms.

With a bestial grunt, Cutter lunged again and thrust the sword through the chair. The blade flashed past his ear and sliced off a few of Rush's hairs. He dropped the heavy clumsy chair as Cutter swung at him again, lopping off the top of a nearby candle.

That could've been my neck!

He rocketed past Cutter and toward a waist-high barrel covered with a silk tablecloth and golden plates. He swept the plates onto the ground, hoping to distract the pirate. Cutter ignored them and advanced on his victim.

Cutter laughed madly. "I've looked forward to this!" he bellowed, slashing the saber back and forth. "I haven't skewered anyone in nearly two hundred years!"

He lunged, thrusting the sword at Rush's belly. In blind panic, Rush scampered like a mouse past the man, nearly colliding with his massive chest.

Cutter lunged again and watched Rush run. The big man laughed and swept a flagon of ale up off a barrel in one massive paw. He hurled the drink down. "I'm enjoying this," he declared, ready to strike again.

Rush dove down and scrambled into an alcove, which was partially blocked behind suitcase-size wooden crates overflowing with pearls and tapestries. He hid, sitting against a rock ledge near the back of the alcove, panting in terror.

What can I do? He'll kill me! But I can't leave Max here—

"You're forgetting, lad," came a voice from behind him.

Rush turned. He saw Dr. Vink on the ledge,

117

crawling toward him from behind a crimson drape. *I thought you were gone!*

"The dagger," Dr. Vink whispered, shaking a golden goblet at Rush's belt. "Use the dagger!" he hissed, and ducked back behind the drape.

Rush pulled the dagger from his belt and looked at it. So tiny, but it had gotten rid of Mr. Noise.

From behind the crates, Rush peered into the treasure room. Cutter was not in sight. The chair where he had sat and whittled was empty.

In a low crouch, his knees bent and his head down, Rush sneaked forward. Dr. Vink poked his head out from behind the drape and watched him go.

Holding the dagger before him, Rush inched along as quietly as he could. The only sound that he could hear was his own husky breathing and the hard quick drumbeat of his blood pounding in his temples. He stayed near the ground, nearly crawling, keeping the dagger low.

Where's Cutter? he thought. *He's gotta be out there somewhere.*

An idea struck that shot a chill up Rush's spine. *What if he's behind me?* Rush looked over his shoulder, still holding the dagger out in front of him.

Cutter's boot stamped on the hand holding the knife.

118

The impact sent Rush tumbling forward. He lay with his face in the cold dirt as the bearlike pirate stood over him. Cutter's boot pressed down hard. Its rough, grimy sole scraped Rush's skin.

Cutter glared down at him, full of contempt. In a bright fast blur, the tip of his sword flew down toward Rush's dagger and flicked it across the room. The dagger flew high and landed in the dusty ground near Max's birdcage.

Cutter let Rush pull his hand out from under the grimy boot. Rush scrambled backward. Before he could get to his feet, he bumped up against a heavy crate that blocked any escape. Cutter stood before him, cornering him like a cat chasing a mouse.

With rising terror, Rush looked up at the buccaneer's glowering face. The big man was no longer amused. He focused on the teenager with raw hatred.

"Is this it?" Cutter rumbled. His lips curled into a scowl of disgust. In a mean, mocking tone, he said, "Is this the grand battle I've been waitin' for?"

Rush had no answer.

"Get up and fight!" Cutter commanded.

"I can't!" Rush cried. "I don't know what to do!"

"Defend yourself!" Cutter roared. Dripping

119

sarcasm, the pirate ghost added, "Like the hero you're supposed to be."

"But I'm not a hero!" Rush wailed.

Cutter glowered at him silently. Rush's gut tightened. He could barely breathe.

Cutter spoke in a slow growl. "Then there's nothin' left for me to do"—he raised his sword high—"but to put you out of my misery." As Rush watched with terrified eyes, Jonas Cutter raised his saber and prepared to slice.

"I don't think so," came a high voice from behind Cutter. The big man turned.

Max shoved himself out of the birdcage. The ropes that had locked the door hung limply from the bars, untied. The boy held Rush's dagger straight up in one steady fist. "Leave him alone!"

Rush scrambled to his feet. Darting around Cutter's vast bulk, he raced toward his brother and stood alongside him. He wasn't sure whether to be grateful that Max had saved him or scared that Max would get himself killed. He reached for the dagger.

"Oh, *two* boys," Cutter mewled in a soft voice. He smiled as if Max and Rush were the cutest things he'd ever seen.

Rush stopped and watched Cutter, worried. *What now?*

"Two boys," Cutter repeated in a soothing tone, and smiled wider. He circled around the room, watching the brothers. Again, he cooed, "Two boys," and slowly spread his arms. If he hadn't been holding a long needle-sharp blade, he would have looked like a loving father inviting his children into a welcoming hug.

Then he lost control. His smile fell into a vicious scowl; he looked not like a loving father but a vulture unfurling its wings to swoop down and kill a prairie dog. "Two *dead* little boys!" he shouted.

Max gulped, his courage fading.

Cutter swung the sword down and pointed its curved blade at Rush, who imagined the sharpened tip ripping him open from belly to jaw in one sweeping stroke. Cutter gripped the handle tight and leaned forward. "Who wants to go first?"

Rush glanced at the dagger in Max's hand and remembered what it did to Mr. Noise. A confident grin slid over his face.

"You do!" he answered.

He took the dagger from Max and held it high, aiming it at Cutter's broad muscular torso. The dagger began to glow and shake.

A blinding white light leaped out, striking Cutter dead center. It ranged all over his body, reaching down his legs and up his chest, spreading like spilled milk from an overturned glass.

The blow sent Cutter stumbling backward as if a hundred fists were punching him. Grunting in agony, he dropped his sword and fell into a chair near the cave wall. To steady himself, Cutter clutched the chair's arms.

That was a mistake. Invisible hands emerged from the chair, pulling thick woody vines behind them. They pulled the vines around Cutter's wrists and tied them around his wrists, between his fingers, and over his mighty biceps, binding them to the arms of the chair. With the ease of tying shoelaces, they wrapped Cutter's torso to the chair's tufted back. They wound around and around, overlapping each other, until he was locked down tight.

Rush gawked at the spectacle. "How'd you do that?" Max asked.

Rush looked at the dagger in his hand and tried to figure out the answer. Only one thought came to mind: "The dagger has the power."

"Good show, lad!" Rush looked up. Dr. Vink was strolling up from behind the brothers, beaming. The stout little occultist raised a finger, pointed it at Rush, and commanded, "There's only one thing left to do."

Max stared at this strange being, with his or-

122

ganlike voice, wild hair, and eyes so intense that they almost glowed. "Who are you?" Max asked.

Dr. Vink ignored him. The gnomish man turned grim as he instructed Rush, "You must run him through with the dagger and fulfill your destiny."

Cutter grinned at them. Although bound by dozens of vines, he jerked his gigantic body from side to side, shaking the chair. The vines didn't snap, but they quivered and stretched, and they didn't look so strong to Rush anymore. If the colossal brute were to break loose, all three of them would die.

"Run me through?" Cutter asked. He laughed as Rush stared. *Doesn't anything stop this guy?*

Cutter smirked at Rush. "The pup doesn't have it in him."

The dagger felt heavy in Rush's hand. *Killing someone . . . do I really have to? I'm only a kid!* He turned to Dr. Vink. "He's right. I can't do that."

Dr. Vink shot Rush a quizzical look. He seemed unable to believe Rush's words. It was as if Rush had announced that he decided to quit eating. "But you must," he insisted. "It's your destiny." He gave Rush a light punch on the shoulder—a bit of manly encouragement.

123

Rush looked back at Cutter. *Can I do it? Will he let me? What if he gets loose?*

The pirate lowered his gaze and focused on Rush like a bull about to charge. He grinned. "Come on, skipper!" he blared. "Use the dagger." He let out a quick swirl of laughter. "You cannot hurt me," he added. Still laughing, he bellowed, "I'm already dead!"

Dr. Vink clapped Rush's shoulder with a heavy hand. He was no longer the clownish, excitable loon that he had seemed before. He was gruff now, hard as a drill sergeant. With a blunt roughness to match Cutter himself, Dr. Vink ordered, "Go on, lad. Use it!"

Rush turned back to Cutter. As Max and Dr. Vink watched, he slowly approached his victim. *Can I really kill him?*

Should I? Do I really want to be a murderer— *like him?*

Cutter saw the uncertainty on Rush's face and heard his heavy nervous breathing. The big man grinned again, as if he were the one bearing down on Rush.

"You won't do it, will ya?" Cutter said.

Stop it, Rush thought. He stepped forward slowly.

Cutter's wide sneer pushed up his cheeks and

124

turned his eyes into fierce slits. "You're just a scared, li'l boy," he teased.

That's not fair. Shut up.

But Cutter kept taunting. "Now, ya fear the dagger." Rush set his mouth in a determined frown and forced himself to get nearer. "But your fear should be of me." Cutter snickered. "For I'll be comin' after ya, skipper!"

Stop it. I don't want to kill you. I don't want to kill anybody!

Rush kept moving, forcing himself to ignore Cutter, to ignore his own qualms, to ignore the gust of cold fear rising from his gut. Cutter's eyes brightened with pleasure. "But before that," he snapped, firing each word like a bullet, "I'll get your little brother!"

"No!" Rush howled, all of the pain and anger and worry of the past two days boiling to the surface. *Not* my *brother, you creep! I'm gonna take care of him no matter what! You want me to stab you?*

You've got it!

He swung the dagger high, ready to jam it into Cutter's face. The pirate hurled his head back, laughing more joyfully than ever.

Rush stopped. He stared into space. *Something's wrong here.*

In mid-laugh, Cutter froze. His eyes widened

125

and his grinning mouth went slack. He stared at Rush.

"What's the trouble, lad?" Dr. Vink asked. The harshness had drained out of his voice; he sounded fatherly, concerned.

Rush lowered the dagger slowly and looked thoughtful. Blinking repeatedly, as if awakening from a second bad dream, he recited, " 'What he wants is not what he desires.' "

Max scrunched up his face in curiosity. "Huh?"

Dr. Vink said nothing. He watched Rush with intense interest.

Cutter, breathing heavily, leaned forward as far as he could and listened raptly.

"That's what Ian's ghost said," Rush continued. He let the hand carrying the dagger drop to his waist as he wrinkled his brow in thought.

"He was a fool," Cutter proclaimed in a voice full of contempt. Rush looked at him, curious. Cutter nodded eagerly. "Finish. Finish the deed!"

"No!" Rush shouted. Suddenly annoyed, he looked away from Cutter's bloodthirsty face. "This isn't right."

Cutter studied Rush for a moment, looking for a weakness. "You're afraid, aren't ya?"

"Yeah. I am," Rush agreed firmly, staring down at the pirate. It felt good. He started to see his

126

idea more clearly, as if approaching it through a fog. "And I think you are, too."

Cutter's eyes widened. His mouth hung open, but he said nothing. Rush went on, "You've been guarding this treasure, but there's no one to guard it from." He suddenly understood: "That's why you took Max, to make sure I would come. You wanted one last battle."

Cutter rallied. "Nonsense talk!" he cried in a harsh shout that used to terrify hard-bitten sailors of a dozen nations. "Use the dagger!" he commanded, but his eyes were alarmed.

Rush kept boring in, punching the pirate with words. "This treasure's no good to you anymore, is it?" he went on. From behind him, Dr. Vink and Max approached. In an accusing tone, Rush went on. "But you have to guard it forever."

A melodic voice said, "I believe you're right, lad." Rush turned to find Dr. Vink at his shoulder. Max stood nearby. Dr. Vink said, "Use the dagger, and Cutter's wretched soul may be released from this prison."

Rush looked back at Cutter. "I get it now. Everything you did—kidnapping Max, making me fall through the trapdoor, fighting me in here— you weren't trying to hurt me. I always had a warning before anything happened, even the spikes and the cannonball in the tunnel. You were just trying to make me so scared and mad that I'd use the dagger on you without even thinking about it."

Cutter whipped his head from side to side. "No!" he howled. "It's not true!" As he thrashed about, the vines around him shivered and jumped but didn't break. Max stepped behind Rush's shoulder for protection from the wild man.

Rush looked at the man, at the dagger in his hand, and at Dr. Vink. "What do I do?"

Dr. Vink backed away from him. As serious as a prophet declaring the fate of a nation, Dr. Vink proclaimed, "Justice for Cutter's victims is in your hands." He pointed at Rush and continued to retreat. "Use it wisely," he said. The words echoed in the big room.

But how? Rush wondered. He felt small and very young. *How can I help people who died two hundred years ago?*

Max watched Rush, wondering what he would do. Rush took the dagger in both hands and looked at it. He turned to Cutter.

The pirate's face was twisted in fury. "Use it!" he screamed. He shoved himself toward Rush as far as he could, straining against the vines. "Use it, blast ya!" the man shrieked. *"Use it!"*

Rush held the dagger carefully, one hand on the handle, one on the blade. He glanced up at

Cutter as the big man writhed in his chair, concentrating his stare on Rush as if to control him by sheer willpower.

Rush looked down at the dagger again. He couldn't stand it anymore.

He gritted his teeth and gripped the dagger harder with both hands. In one fast stroke, he cracked it over his knee.

The blade broke off neatly from the handle. Both pieces dropped to the floor and lay amid a few gold coins on a Chinese carpet.

The pieces started to glow and rose to a blinding brilliance; as it faded, Rush was amazed to see that the blade and handle once again looked as ancient and scruffy as when he had first seen them. The power was drained out of them.

Cutter stared at the pieces. He shook his head wildly, refusing to believe that Rush had destroyed his last chance. "Curse ya!" he wailed. "Curse ya all!"

With a low rumble, the treasure room began to vibrate and shimmy. Rush's jaw fell as he gawked at the shuddering walls. "The dagger has the power." But this much power?

A spiderweb of thin black fissures spread through the ceiling and down the walls. Dust and gravel fell from the cracks.

"It's caving in!" Rush shouted.

129

CHAPTER 14

The two brothers swung around, looking for Dr. Vink.

"Where'd he go?" asked Max. The strange little man was nowhere in sight, but the door to the tunnel was open. Had Dr. Vink escaped through it?

Beneath the boys' feet, the ground quivered and roared. *Sorry, Dr. Vink,* Rush thought, *but we've gotta get outta here!* "C'mon," Rush ordered, grabbing Max's wrist. They ran for the door.

Shielding their heads from falling gravel, Max and Rush stumbled and ran. The tunnel of the gauntlet rocked wildly, shaking harder than the treasure room. Boulders the size of basketballs crashed around them. *We're not gonna make it!* Rush thought.

Cutter shook, helplessly entangled in the vines. "Cowards!" he roared as the room thrashed and enormous stones fell. "Yer all cowards! Cowards all!"

Rush and Max ran past the spikes and the hanging skeleton, the ground leaping in sharp jolts, the air clogged with dust. Falling branches and pebbles pelted them. Staggering and coughing, Rush squinted into the rain of rocks before him. He kept running, with Max close behind.

The treasure room rattled and bounced as its ceiling split apart. "No!" Cutter screamed. "No, don't leave me here!"

Rocks and chips from the ceiling pounded Rush's head. With Max at his back, he stumbled into the big chamber with the trapdoor.

Rush spotted a vine that hung down from the door's hinges, and next to the vine, he saw the rickety ladder that he had noticed when he first entered the room. *Freedom!* he thought.

"Go!" Rush shouted, pushing his brother up the ladder's shaky rungs. Spiky shards broke off the cave wall; Rush ducked as they fell past his ears.

"No!" Cutter begged as boulders cascaded down on him. "Please don't leave me alone!" A flood of man-size ceiling shards showered over his trapped body. The pirate ghost let out an agonized final howl.

In the big chamber, the ladder quavered and jumped as Max climbed. Halfway up, Max looked down at Rush, standing at the base of the ladder and trying to hold it steady. The nearby vine, swinging with every quake, flew across Rush's face like a whip.

As rocks rained down, Rush forced himself to look up. *Keep going, Max!* Rush glanced around—no Cutter in sight, no Dr. Vink—and looked back up at his brother.

He paid no attention to a thin gray cord nearby, brittle and frayed with age—the only thing connecting the ladder to the wall.

As the cavern jumped and jolted, the cord pulled tight and sagged. A dozen of its threads snapped.

Again, the ground shook. The cord loosened and lost more threads. It was as thin as kite string, and getting thinner.

Max gripped the rungs tight and continued to climb, trying to ignore the rocks falling past him and the ladder jumping under his feet. He reached up through the trapdoor and clutched the edge of the mausoleum floor.

132

The air was clean up there, filled with moonlight rather than choking dust. He pulled himself onto the cool smooth concrete.

Rush looked around again for Cutter and Dr. Vink. A jolt hit, sending down a waterfall of stones onto his head. The vine hanging next to the ladder swung into his eyes.

"C'mon!" Max called through the trapdoor. "Hurry!"

Rush pulled himself up the rungs as the ladder rocked and wobbled. Stones poured down onto his hands, nearly knocking them off the ladder. *Don't fall*, he told himself. *Don't fall, don't fall, don't fall!*

He didn't see the weak gray cord snap tight and sag and snap tight again as the earthquake raged on. A dozen more threads split.

The ladder whipped back and forth like a flag in a hurricane, yanking on the fragile cord. The nearby vine scratched his cheek. Rush hung on and kept climbing. *Don't fall!*

The cord broke. The ladder plummeted backward into the roaring hailstorm of rocks, taking Rush with it. He saw the ground careening toward him.

I'm going to die!

He grabbed the hanging vine. He looked up; the vine was hanging from the trapdoor. *I can climb up!*

133

Another quake hit, slamming Rush into the craggy rock wall, but he held on, dangling and swinging as the room shook.

The ladder clattered on the stone floor. Rocks crashed down and shattered the fragile rungs where Rush had been standing. He gripped the vine and careened helplessly.

Max reached down to grab him, but the young boy was too short. No matter how much Max stretched and strained, his fingers wouldn't reach.

"Grab my hand!" Max yelled.

Rush pulled himself up the vine, hand over hand, trying not to feel the scratchy harsh hemp cut into the soft flesh of his palm and fingers. Another earthquake shook the room, smashing his face into the wall. He grimaced and pulled himself up.

Max lay on his belly, pushing himself down into the chamber as far as he could, holding the corner of the trapdoor with one hand to keep himself from falling. His arm ached from the strain of reaching for Rush. Lines of hot sharp pain burned up his outstretched fingers.

One more inch, Rush thought. He yanked himself up the vine. In desperation, he let one hand go and swung it upward.

It slapped into Max's open palm.

Rush closed his fingers over Max's thin wrist and clasped tight. *I'm gonna live!*

134

"I got you!" Max said. "Hang on!"

The boy grunted. The strain of pulling his big brother up was too much. Max held tight to Rush and to the floor, terrified of dropping into the deadly cavern.

Max strained every muscle, clutching Rush's wrist, but Rush was too heavy. Max pulled his knees up under his chest for balance and let go of the trapdoor, grabbing Rush's wrist with both hands. "C'mon," Max pleaded.

Max's hands crawled along Rush's arm to pull more of him up. He tightened every muscle down to his toes and pulled.

Rush slowly hauled up the vine and through the trapdoor. He reached out his free hand and touched the mausoleum floor.

"Gotcha!" Max yelled.

Rush crawled into the mausoleum. *I made it!* For a wild second, he wanted to kiss the floor.

"Come on!" Max shouted. The two boys ran out into the cool night air. They tumbled to the grass, exhausted and panting.

The door to the mausoleum shut behind them. All was silent. The earthquakes were over.

"Grandson?" came a familiar voice.

CHAPTER
15

The brothers whirled to see the ghost of Ian Keegan standing in the moonlight. They jumped to their feet and faced him, their mouths hanging open.

No longer was Ian the desperate, exhausted wraith that Rush had seen. It seemed to Rush that the victory over Cutter had soothed him. The ghost stood calm and confident as he waited for the boys to steady themselves.

The ghost smiled warmly. "I'm proud of you," he said in a voice stronger than Rush had heard him use before. While Max gaped at the dead man, Rush searched for a reply.

Finally, he asked, "Did I do the right thing?"

The ghost nodded gently. "The dagger was meant to punish Cutter for his evil ways, and that's what was done." He smiled again, more widely than before. For a dead man, he looked fairly lively. "Aye. Ye did the right thing."

A welcome gust of relief swept through Rush. He felt calmer than he had in days. Still, he needed to know more. "Thanks, but why didn't you tell me what Cutter was up to? That 'what he wants is not what he desires'—I didn't know what you meant till the last second. And why didn't you tell me how to use the dagger? All I knew was that it had power." Suddenly Rush had a ton of questions.

The ghost shook his head sadly. "I'm sorry, grandson. I didn't know how to use it myself. The dagger and spyglass and key were enchanted not just with my own hopes and dreams, but with the yearning spirits of all who died by Cutter's cruel hand. I did not know how their wishes would affect the dagger.

"Nor did I know what Cutter would do. No doubt, he would try to fool you into doing what he desired. But exactly how he would go about it, I could not say." The ghost smiled sheepishly. "I never could predict him. If I could, he would never have murdered me." He grew serious again. "Besides, 'tis not easy for spirits to contact the living—that is why ghosts are rare. I told you all I could before I had to fade away."

The ghost looked from one brother to the other. "Handsome boys." He leaned down toward them as if about to impart a precious secret. "Quite the family resemblance."

Rush and Max looked at each other. Did he mean that they resembled each other or him?

The dead man stood up straight and smiled again. "Farewell, grandsons." He winked and began to disappear. "Thank you," he whispered, and was gone.

Rush stared at the spot where Ian had stood, trying to sort out all that had happened. It was too much for him to handle alone. He laid an arm around Max's shoulders.

"Man," Max whispered, "this is the strangest."

Rush looked at him and thought, *Got that right, little bro.*

He noticed something odd at Max's feet: the spyglass. *That's weird. I must've dropped it when I went into the mausoleum.*

He picked it up, pulled out the inside tube, and raised the scope to his eye. He saw the cemetery's tombstones, standing peacefully in the quiet grass.

The next morning, Rush opened and raised the spyglass again, and saw his own home. The old brown tube worked perfectly—as a normal telescope. No longer was it a magic window into another world.

The walk home in the dark had taken hours. Fortunately, Rush remembered the route that Dr. Vink had driven.

Along the way, they went over their entire adventure. Max couldn't understand why he kept calling Rush "Grandson." Keegan wasn't their grandfather; their grandfathers were alive, and Keegan must be their great-great-many-times-great-grandfather. Rush tried to explain that it was only a figure of speech.

The boys now stood on the lawn near the lake shore, discussing their adventure. Should they tell Mom and Dad, or Sandy and Tony, or anyone?

"No one's ever gonna believe us," Max insisted.

Right again, Rush thought. He was about to speak when he heard a familiar voice: "Good show, lads!"

Dr. Vink was approaching them from behind.

"What happened to you?" Rush asked. He wasn't sure whether he was relieved to see that Dr. Vink was alive or annoyed at the old weirdo for running out on him back in the treasure room.

A grin split Dr. Vink's face. He virtually sang his answer. "I thought it best to leave you to your own devices. After all"—he leaned toward Rush and pointed at him—"this is *your* adventure." He straightened up and smiled at Rush with immense pride.

Dr. Vink seemed so happy at the victory and escape that Rush couldn't get mad. After all, the old man did help him rescue Max. "Sorry you didn't get the treasure you wanted," Rush said.

"No matter." Dr. Vink laughed. "Treasure doesn't last." He turned earnest. "It's the adventure, the excitement, the game!" He waggled a finger at them. "That's what stays with you a lifetime. Remember that."

The doctor dipped his hands into his saggy pockets and extended a fist toward each of the boys. In a low secretive tone, he said, "Though a little treasure never hurt, either."

He dropped a dark ruby into Rush's hands and gave Max a sparkling sapphire. The gems were cut flawlessly and glistened in the morning sunlight.

"Wow!" Max gasped. Rush stared in awe. *This guy never stops coming up with surprises.* Rush looked up at Dr. Vink. "Guess you didn't come away empty-handed."

"No. But I did!"

A familiar man in a gypsy blouse, vest, and

140

headscarf strode up behind Max and Rush. Sardo (*No "mister," accent on the "do,"* Rush reminded himself) pointed an accusing finger at Dr. Vink. He ignored the boys as he glared at the scruffy old man.

"We had a deal," Sardo said with quiet anger. In a high furious squeak, he continued, "You ran out on me. It took me all night to track you down here." He closed one eye and pointed at the doctor as if aiming through a rifle sight. "I delivered. Now, I expect you to." He shook with anger, making his billowy sleeves wiggle. Max reached out and tugged the shiny fabric between thumb and forefinger. Sardo jerked the sleeve away.

"Please," Dr. Vink said in a soothing tone. "I intend to double your fee."

Sardo paused. He grinned like a fool, twiddling his chubby fingers as if riffling through thousand-dollar bills. "Double?" he asked.

With a determined look, he shoved past Rush and Max toward the doctor, who seemed vastly amused. "Oh, well, that's different," Sardo continued, his delivery clipped and businesslike.

He noticed bits of lint on Dr. Vink's jacket, and began plucking them off like a loyal butler making sure that his beloved master would look his best. In a chummy voice, he went on, "Maybe we could, uh . . ."

A car horn beeped. Rush knew the sound immediately.

"Mom and Dad!" Max shouted. He sprinted toward the house with Rush behind him.

Rush stopped and headed back toward the two men. "I don't know who you guys are"—the men looked at him, and Sardo stopped grooming Dr. Vink—"but I don't think I'll ever forget you." Rush smiled. For a second, he just looked at them, memorizing their faces, then he took off after Max.

Dr. Vink smiled fondly and watched Rush go. Sardo watched, too, but he was busily calculating. As soon as Rush was out of sight, Sardo laid a hand on Dr. Vink's shoulder and showed him an oily smirk. "Listen . . ." he began in the sneaky tone that car salesmen use to pass off broken-down junkers as valuable classics.

Dr. Vink scowled. He shrugged Sardo's hand off and walked away. Sardo called after him, "What other little adventures do you think we might be able to cook up together?"

Dr. Vink kept walking. Sardo trotted after him, still talking.

*   *   *

142

With Rush behind him, Max raced into the driveway. Their parents were getting out of the station wagon.

"Mom! Dad!" Max shouted happily. He hurled himself at his mother. Flinging his arms around her, Max squeezed his eyes shut and clutched her tight.

"Whoa! What's this about?" she asked, peeling him off.

Rush jogged to a stop. "You're never gonna believe this, but—"

"No, you're never gonna believe this," Mom declared. "We had the most"—she searched for a word—"*amazing* weekend." She seemed light-headed, and danced into the house.

Dad circled around from the other side of the car, a knapsack slung over his shoulder. He watched Mom go. "Wait'll we tell ya," he said to the boys, clapping Max on the shoulder. "It's the most unbelievable thing you ever heard." Chuckling to himself, Dad followed his wife into the house.

Max sighed. Didn't anyone want to hear their story? He leaned weakly against the car and looked up at Rush. "Are we gonna tell them?"

Rush eyed the spyglass in his hand. He pulled it open. Would they believe the story? Would they even want to hear it?

143

He snapped the spyglass shut. "I don't think so," Rush said. "It'll be our secret." Rush smiled down at his little brother. Max smiled back.

Rush led Max into the old familiar house. Just before they went in the door, Rush smiled and slung an arm around his brother's shoulder.

Epilogue: The Midnight Society

Rush and Max never told anyone about their adventure because they were afraid someone might look for Cutter's treasure.

And if they found it, they'd also find the ghost of the pirate captain, lying in wait for one last battle.

Sardo went back to his shop, and Dr. Vink—well, he just vanished. They say that he continues to wander the earth, luring new allies into dangerous situations.

So if you run into a little man with dancing eyes and an echoing voice . . . you'd better run the other way.

And that's our tale. I officially declare this meeting of the Midnight Society closed.

ARE YOU AFRAID OF THE DARK?

As for you, visitor, you're always welcome in our storytelling circle. We meet here as soon as darkness falls.

It should be perfectly safe. Of course, as Rush found out, frightening things happen in the darkness.

So come back any time . . . if you can face one question:

Are you afraid of the dark?

ABOUT THE AUTHOR

David L. Seidman has written for virtually every kind of publication, from newspapers to coloring books. He has worked as a comic-book editor, a teacher, a publishing consultant, and an improvisational comedian. He lives in West Hollywood, California, with his cat, Killer.

YOU COULD WIN A TRIP TO NICKELODEON STUDIOS!

1 Grand Prize: A weekend(4 day/3 night)trip to Nickelodeon Studios in Orlando, FL
3 First Prizes: A Nickelodeon collection of ten videos
25 Second Prizes: A Clarissa board game
50 Third Prizes: One year subscription to Nickelodeon Magazine

Name_____Birthdate_____

Address_____

City_____State_____Zip_____

Daytime Phone_____

POCKET BOOKS/"Win a trip to Nickelodeon Studios" SWEEPSTAKES
Sweepstakes Sponsors Official Rules:

1. No Purchase Necessary. Enter by submitting the completed Official Entry
Form (no copies allowed) or by sending on a 3" x 5" card your name and
address to the Pocket Books/Nickelodeon Sweepstakes, Advertising and
Promotion Department, 13th Floor, 1230 Avenue of the Americas, NY, NY
10020. Entries must be received by 12/29/95. Not responsible for lost, late
or misdirected mail or for typographical errors in the entry form or rules.
Enter as often as you wish, but one entry per envelope. Winners will be
selected at random from all entries received in a drawing to be held on or
about 1/2/96.

2. Prizes: One Grand Prize: A weekend (four day/three night) trip for up to
four persons (the winning minor, one parent or legal guardian and two
guests) including round-trip coach airfare from the major U.S. airport nearest
the winner's residence, ground transportation or car rental, meals, three
nights in a hotel (one room, occupancy for four) and a tour of Nickelodeon
Studios in Orlando, Florida (*approx. retail value $3500.00*), Three First
Prizes: A Nickelodeon collection of ten videos (*approx. retail value $200.00
each*), Twenty-Five Second Prizes: A Clarissa board game (*approx. retail
value $15.00 each*), Fifty Third Prizes: One year subscription to

Nickelodeon magazine (*approx. retail value $18.00 each*).

3. The sweepstakes is open to residents of the U.S. and Canada no older than fourteen as of 12/29/95. Proof of age required to claim prize. Prizes will be awarded to the winner's parent or legal guardian. Void in Puerto Rico and wherever else prohibited or restricted by law. Employees of Viacom International Inc., their suppliers, subsidiaries, affiliates, agencies, participating retailers, and their families living in the same household are not eligible.

4. One prize per person or household. Prizes are not transferable and may not be substituted. All prizes will be awarded. The odds of winning a prize depend upon the number of entries received.

5. If a winner is a Canadian resident, then he/she must correctly answer a skill-based question administered by mail. Any litigation respecting the conduct and awarding of a prize in this publicity contest may be submitted to the Regie des Loteries et Courses du Quebec.

6. All federal, state and local taxes are the responsibility of the winners. Winners will be notified by mail. Winners may be required to execute and return an Affidavit of Eligibility and Release and all other legal documents which the sweepstakes sponsor may require (including a W-9 tax form) within 15 days of notification or an alternate winner will be selected.

7. Winners grant Pocket Books and MTV Networks the right to use their names, likenesses, and entries for any advertising, promotion and publicity purposes without further compensation to or permission from the entrants, except where prohibited by law.

8. Winners agree that Viacom International Inc., its parent, subsidiaries and affiliated companies, or any sponsors, as well as the employees of each of these, shall have no liability in connection with the collection, acceptance or use of the prizes awarded herein.

9. By participating in this sweepstakes, entrants agree to be bound by these rules and the decisions of the judges and sweepstakes sponsors, which are final in all matters relating to the sweepstakes.

10. For a list of major prize winners, (available after 1/2/96) send a stamped, self-addressed envelope to Prize Winners, Pocket Books/Nickelodeon Sweepstakes Advertising and Promotion Department, 13th Floor, 1230 Avenue of the Americas, NY, NY 10020